The Month of Zephram Mondays

*The very first of the
Zephram Tales*

by
Leslie A. Susskind

Good Manners
Kids Stuff Press

This book is an original publication of
Good Manners Kids Stuff Press

ISBN-10 0-9824744-1-5
ISBN-13 978-0-9824744-1-9

Interested in more good manners books and products?
Please visit us at:
www.goodmannerskidsstuff.com
www.goodmannerskidsstuffpress.com
Because good manners might just make the world a better place!™

Dedicated to:
Bill, Paige, Rebecca
and our family and friends
for their support
and encouragement!

Leslie Aurandt Susskind has worked for years
in advertising and marketing and is excited
to be living her life-long dream:
writing children's books!

A busy mom, Leslie lives with her
husband, Bill, and two daughters outside of
Philadelphia, Pennsylvania.

Please check with Amazon and
Good Manners Kids Stuff Press for
more of Leslie's books coming soon,
including "The Kids' (and parents, too!)
Book of Good Sportsmanship,"
available December 2009, and the second book
in the Zephram series,
"The Tale of Time Warp Tuesday,"
available Fall 2010.

www.goodmannerskidsstuffpress.com
www.zephramtales.com
www.lesliesusskind.com

The Month of
Zephram Mondays

Chapter One

"I hate Mondays!"

Back in the days when there were dragons and knights and three-headed ogres, and wizards and fairies and hydroxes, and a lot of other kinds of interesting things, the Royal Quadruplets of the Kingdom of Zephram glumly gathered in the Royal Schoolroom for a long, Zephram Monday, spent learning important Royal Subjects.

The Royal Quadruplets' names were Thomasin, Lizeta, Nedwyn and Elenlyn, but since they weren't quite grown up yet (and their names were sort of hard to say), most people called them Tom, Lizzie, Ned and Nell. And, of course, they were also called Prince or Princess too, because that was what they were.

"I hate Mondays," Ned grumbled again, for it was Ned who could always be counted on to complain. "Just because stupid old King Otto thought Zephram Mondays were a great idea a thousand years ago, I don't know why *we* still have to do it. No other country has to do it."

His brother and sisters ignored him because they heard the same thing *every* Monday! Monday was the day when *everything* everyone did was dedicated or donated to Zephram for the upkeep and support of the kingdom.

It didn't matter what type of job the people did, whether they were bakers, or jewelers, or carpenters, or horse trainers, or doctors, or math teachers. Whatever the Zephramites earned, made, or did on the other days of the week was theirs to keep. But on Mondays, all work was for the good of the country. That meant that even school children took their tests on Mondays so that they got in the habit of working hard on Mondays when they grew up.

The proceeds and donations from Zephram Mondays paid for important things such as the military and the college and the hospital and the orphanage, so that everyone in the kingdom was taken care of: happy, healthy, and able to become as smart as they ever wanted to be!

During today's Zephram Monday, the Royal Quadruplets were supposed to be hard at work studying for their Weekly Test, just as they did every Monday. But the Royal Tutor hadn't arrived yet, so Nell and Lizzie were talking about their sister Princess Zephera's upcoming marriage to Duke Harry *and* their father King Hiram's 50th birthday celebration, both of which were going to be held in a month's time on the same day. Ned, as usual, was complaining and trying to cause trouble. Only Tom was quietly concentrating on a big, musty, leather-bound book.

"Duke Harry is ever so handsome," sighed Lizzie about their sister's fiancé. "I hope that when I am as old as Zephera, I can marry a prince or a king or a duke just as nice."

"Fat chance," joked Ned, who was trying to annoy his sister just as any brother would.

"And I'll wear a wedding gown that is covered in pearls and lace," she continued, ignoring him just as any sister would. "And I'll have flowers in my hair, and a flora-ora tiara with diamonds on it. Why, I think it will be even prettier than the diamond necklace Zephera wants."

"You'll never find anyone like Duke Harry to marry you," said Ned, again trying his best to annoy her. "He's the bravest warrior there ever was. Besides, someone like him wouldn't ever even *talk* to you."

Lizzie continued to ignore him. "And I'd have eight white horses pull my carriage, and my carriage would be made of gold and silver and have real diamonds and other sparkly stuff all around the windows. All the people will be throwing flora-ora confetti as we drive past – wouldn't that be just lovely?"

"Flora-ora confetti," her sister, Nell, repeated approvingly. "I love that idea. Now that would be a nice touch." Nell was busy admiring the shocking green flora-ora polish she had just applied to her nails. "But won't you have to move away when you get married? Live in *his* castle?"

"I don't know," admitted Lizzie. "Eeuwh, that would be awful. Well, our castle is quite large enough.

We could all live here forever and ever. It's so big, we'd never have to even see <u>you</u>," she said, glaring at Ned.

"You'll be living here forever and ever anyway, because no one will want to marry you," Ned retorted. Then he changed his tone. "Well, I'm not getting married. Gross. Who needs a silly girlfriend?"

"Well, no silly girl would want *you* anyway!" Nell jumped into the conversation to defend and support Lizzie as any *good* sister would. "You're so nasty! I bet Dad sends you off to patrol the borders as soon as you're old enough. No one wants you around."

"I can't *wait* to go," Ned declared, pleased to have gotten reactions from both of his sisters. "Who wants to be around –"

"Come on, stop it!" said Tom, finally looking up from his book. Tom was the only one *really* studying hard for their Weekly Test – not only because he was the first one of the quadruplets to be born (he beat Lizzie by 11 minutes), but because he was also the oldest boy, and going to be Zephram's king one day. Understandably, he took his heritage very seriously. He knew that he would have to know all kinds of answers when he ruled the kingdom. Passing The Test was *really* important for him to do.

Ned made a face at Nell and Lizzie, and then went over to the window to toy around with the telescope that was set up there. He pointed the telescope away from the water harbor views to look over the forests, hills and dales of Zephram. He could see forever, and imagined himself far, far away from the Royal Schoolroom on this boring Zephram Monday.

"You really should be studying this, too," Tom said, pointing at his book.

"Maybe they'll forget," said Ned, not even looking away from the telescope.

"Like that ever happens, especially on a Monday," said Tom, shaking his head in exasperation at his brother.

"Ned, why are you looking through that thing?" Nell wasn't about to give up annoying him, especially since he'd started it. "You're only supposed to use it at night."

"No, that's not true," said Ned. "I can use it anytime and anyway I want. Besides, I might not be looking at just the stars and moon. Who knows what I'll see if I look in the right place?" Ned slowly panned the telescope around to show how busy he was. "Hey, what's that?" he asked a few minutes later. "I just saw a flash. Did you see one?"

Tom, Nell and Lizzie said no.

"There it is again," Ned said. "Um – it looks like people are unloading a boat at the back of the harbor. Maybe it's the sun reflecting on a piece of metal?"

"Maybe," Tom agreed absently. There was a knock at the door.

"Come in," Lizzie called.

"Excuse me, your Highnesses," said the Royal Tutor's Assistant, standing in the doorway. "I have the latest delivery of the *History of Ancient Zephram* pages for your *History of Ancient Zephram* History Book." The *History of Ancient Zephram* was like a 'real time' history, written by the History Writer and delivered current-event-fresh each week.

"Thank you," said Lizzie, rising up to take the stack from him since he didn't seem to want to enter the room. But the Royal Tutor's Assistant wasn't quite finished with his errand.

"I have been asked to let you know the Royal Tutor has the flu –"

"Woo hoo!" Ned loudly whooped with glee, while Nell whispered a delighted, "Yes!"

"And he told me to tell you to be sure to spend your Zephram Monday time studying about the invasion of Hilden for a quiz tomorrow," the Royal Tutor's Assistant continued, frowning at Ned and Nell.

"Oh, great," Ned grumbled.

"Of course we will," Lizzie assured him (Lizzie was always unfailingly polite). "Please tell the Royal Tutor we are studying hard and hope he feels better."

"Hardly studying," Ned whispered to Nell.

"Thank *you*, Princess," said the Royal Tutor's Assistant to Lizzie, and he backed quickly out of the doorway, his job done.

"*Please tell him we hope he feels better,*" Ned mimicked his sister as the door closed. "I should say <u>not</u>. Who wants to study *more*?"

"More? Try at all," Nell suggested, her small moment of bonding with Ned over.

Tom was glancing over the new pages the Royal Tutor's Assistant had brought. "Looks like last week's Treaty is in here, all up-to-date." He put the pages carefully at the end of the big huge ancient book that had been manhandled by the Royal Children – and all their ancestors, in fact – for the last thousand years. Then, the quadruplets finally settled in for a relatively quiet period of studying (or in Ned's case, whatever else he could find to do instead).

"Now, about our gift for Dad's birthday," Lizzie said presently, looking up from her book. "I was thinking we could –"

Suddenly, the sound of a gong was heard. The quadruplets jumped at the noise and looked at each other in dismay.

"Oh *dear*," said Lizzie, biting her lip.

"Oh *no*," said Nell, looking down at the green flora-ora nail polish that her mother had absolutely forbidden her to wear.

"No *way*," said Ned, turning away from the window and telescope.

"Not *already*," said Tom with dismay, closing his book. Because it was that dreaded time, dreaded by the Royal Quadruplets: the dreaded once-a-week Test Time with their Royal Parents.

"At least *some* of us have been studying," Nell said triumphantly to Ned. "Maybe *some* of us will pass the Test this time!"

"Yeah, right," her brother laughed.

"Let's go get it over with," Tom said, getting up from the table. "Come on."

With glum faces, the quadruplets left the safe boredom of their Royal Schoolroom and slowly made their way through the maze of castle hallways to meet their weekly fate.

"Good morning, your Highnesses," a group of school girls said obediently as they passed each other in the hallway. Then they whispered behind their hands and giggled at Nell and Lizzie because *they* were on their way to recess, and they knew the Royal Quadruplets were on *their* way to take their Weekly Test.

A test that everyone else had passed long ago.

"They are so annoying," said Nell, and Lizzie squeezed her hand in sympathy. The four trudged slowly and steadfastly onward.

"Good morning, your Highnesses," said Alf, the Royal Tailor's son, with a smug smile on his face he directed at Ned as they passed each other. Alf knew what time it was, too.

"He is so annoying. I hate him," said Ned of his arch nemesis.

"Stop it – we don't hate anyone," Tom said.

"Maybe *you* don't," said Nell, "but they don't pull the same stuff on you that they do on us. You're going to be King Thomasin one day – they're not that stupid," she reminded him.

At that moment they arrived at the ornately carved and flora-ora gilded doors of the Royal Throne Room. The quadruplets stopped and looked at each other.

"Dare you to knock," Ned teased his brother.

"The sooner we do it, the sooner we can go," Tom reasoned to Nell and Lizzie, choosing to pay no attention to Ned.

"You're right," Lizzie agreed.

"Coward," Tom said to Ned, and he bravely knocked.

Jepson, the Royal Steward, opened the big doors with a loud creak. He looked down and saw the Royal Quadruplets.

"Their Royal Highnesses Crown Prince Thomasin, Princess Lizeta, Prince Nedwyn and Princess Elenlyn have arrived, your Majesties," he announced. He stepped aside and, with a big flourish of his hand, gestured for them to enter the room.

Test Time had come.

Chapter Two

Their parents, King Hiram and Queen Melora, were waiting for Tom, Lizzie, Ned and Nell inside the vast, grand room. Queen Melora was busy needle-pointing brand new pillows for the throne because the thrones were quite uncomfortable when one sat on them for hours on end (especially on Zephram Mondays). King Hiram had been busy signing his big, kingly signature on all kinds of bills and laws, and he put his pen and papers aside.

They smiled fondly at their Royal Quadruplets – at their four curly blonde heads, their four little freckled noses, their four pairs of mischievous blue eyes and their four gap-toothed smiles (the quadruplets were getting their grownup teeth and Tom even had a retainer that was made out of flora-ora) – *and* they smiled hopefully, too. The four looked so much like their older sister Princess Zephera (who had been a straight A student with her lessons) they felt there was always a chance that good old fashioned book learning would accomplish what Mother Nature hadn't.

"Hello, children," King Hiram greeted them with a smile.

"Hello, Mom and Dad," Tom, Lizzie, Ned and Nell chorused.

"What have you been doing on this fine Zephram Monday?" King Hiram asked.

"Studying," they answered obediently. (As if they'd say anything else!)

"Great!" said their father with a big, encouraging smile. "Glad to hear it. What do you have to show your mother and me today?" Having used a stall and distract routine before to put off the inevitable testing (sometimes even successfully), the quadruplets launched into their familiar roles.

"A song," said Lizzie.

"A dance," said Nell.

"A family tree chart," said Ned.

"A new star," said Tom.

"It sounds as if you've been busy," said King Hiram, willing to let them stall for a few minutes before they took The Test. "Let's start with you, Lizeta."

Lizzie stepped forward, took a deep breath and opened her mouth to sing. Lizzie's voice had a beautiful, sweet, bell-like sound that enchanted everyone who heard it. Her royal parents were mesmerized by her voice as they always were, and showered her with praise when she finished.

"Elenlyn, it's your turn, dear," said Queen Melora gently, several moments later as the echo of Lizzie's last notes faded away. Tom, Lizzie and Ned moved back to give their sister some room.

Nell loved to move so much that she had a hard time keeping still, so it was a good thing that she was blessed with grace, strength and balance. Nell showed her Royal Family her latest routine, which combined ballet and gymnastics. She pirouetted, danced, flipped, and jumped all around the room to an imaginary music track, and ended with a handspring into a split.

"Tah dah!" she cried, as everyone applauded.

"Well done!" said the King.

"Elenlyn, take off that nail polish before dinner," said the eagle-eyed Queen.

"Yes, Mom," Nell said as she carefully backed up and hid her hands (with their green finger nails) behind her back.

"Thomasin, your turn, my boy," said King Hiram.

"I found a new star," Tom said, unrolling a chart to show his parents where it was located.

"How did you do that?" asked King Hiram, impressed.

"When I was looking at the stars a couple of months ago, I noticed something seemed different. So I used a compass and an astrolabe and a telescope to take measurements every night before I was able to figure out last week what was causing it," Tom explained. "Do you think I should name the star for Zephram?"

"I think you should name it after yourself," replied his mother. "You found it, after all."

"Tom Star," snorted Ned.

"Okay," said Tom, rolling his chart back up and giving his brother an evil stare. "Ned, it's *your* turn."

"I learned the names of all the kings and queens of Zephram back to King Otto," Ned said with a mischievous smile. The list would certainly take some time and maybe, just maybe, their test might be forgotten. "In fact, I can do it backwards. Want to hear it? King Hiram and Queen Melora, that's you, Grandpa King Baltius and Grandma Queen Zepherna, Great Granddad ... " he started rattling off the kings' and queens' names without waiting for an answer.

Ten minutes later he ground to a halt. " ... and King Otto," he ended triumphantly.

"All backwards, well, um, interesting," said his mother. "I've never heard it recited that way before. Thank you, Nedwyn."

"Don't you think *all* the school children should learn to do it?" Ned asked, with an evil glint in his eyes that his brother and sisters recognized.

"Possibly," said Kind Hiram, looking interested at the idea. For a split second the four thought that they had successfully diverted attention from –

"Children, as always you've done very well with your school work this week. But your mother and I want to make sure we do The Test before we run out of time."

Nope. Unfortunately for the quadruplets, they *hadn't* diverted their Royal Parents' attention from the stupid dreaded Test.

"Your tutor says you've been working hard, I believe," King Hiram said, referring to the Royal Tutor's notes.

The quadruplets looked at each other with barely disguised agony. The moment of truth had come. It was time for their Weekly Test: not Spelling, not Math, not History, not Science. Those subjects were a breeze for the children (even for Ned, when he concentrated). Unfortunately, their test was on … MAGIC.

"Yes, we have been studying our magic, Dad," Tom said bravely. He knew that he was going to have to be brave when he became king someday, so he forced himself to speak for all of them.

"Excellent," said King Hiram.

"We worked on Disappearing again this week."

"Let's see it – or 'not' see it," King Hiram said, chuckling at his little joke. "You know, disappearing," he added to Queen Melora. She nodded indulgently.

Tom took a moment for Ned and their sisters to get ready. "Okay, here goes."

Each of the quadruplets made a desperate, silent wish, and then held their breaths, closed their eyes and clenched their fists until their cheeks turned purple.

Seconds ticked by.

And ticked by.

And ticked by.

"That's enough," said their concerned father before the four collapsed in front of him from lack of air, since they were, unfortunately, still *there*.

"Sorry," Lizzie gasped, apologizing sheepishly.

The quadruplets looked miserably at each other. They felt horrible at this latest failure of The Test, although they weren't surprised it hadn't worked, because they had been *pretty* sure they weren't going to disappear, no matter how hard they studied. But at least they had gotten it over with. Now they could escape for another week –

"I don't suppose you could try The Chant?" Queen Melora asked, looking wistfully at them.

The four gulped in dismay. It was tough to always be disappointing their mom and dad. But – The Chant?

A good, long, 10 seconds passed (maybe even 20) until dependable Tom stepped forward, *again* accepting his responsibility as the oldest and heir to the throne.

"You all owe me big time," he muttered under his breath to his brother and sisters.

He picked up an impressive looking book from the table next to his father's throne, and held it out in front of him. The other three crossed their fingers as Tom chanted:

"Meena mumbo chah

Krako, mumbo chah

Steeple, mumbo chah,"

and let go of the book. All eyes in the Royal Throne Room were centered on the book, willing, begging, pleading for it to float.

Instead, a split second later it dropped to the floor with a huge thud, just missing Tom's toes by a tiny fraction of an inch. King Hiram cleared his throat as the noise echoed in the silent room.

"Well, um – fine job on your studies," he said, exchanging glances with his wife.

"There's always next week," Queen Melora told them in comforting tones. "We'll just try again."

It was a good thing their older sister, Princess Zephera, chose that moment to poke her pretty blond head into the Royal Throne Room and interrupt the whole sorry meeting.

"Hey, all done?" she asked, looking at their sad faces and seeing the book on the floor next to Tom's feet. She had slipped past Jepson to open the big heavy doors herself, and he followed behind her with apologetic glances to the King and Queen.

"Yes," the quadruplets all said right away before their parents could say anything to the contrary.

"Great!" Princess Zephera said with a big smile. "Mom, why don't I take them with me now, if they're finished."

The quadruplets brightened up immediately – here was their chance to escape from the whole miserable, embarrassing Test before things got any worse and someone got hurt!

"What a perfect idea, Zephera. Run along with your sister, children," said Queen Melora, as Tom picked up the offending book and returned it to the table.

"I hope you'll be working on my birthday surprise," the King called after them, mustering a smile for them in spite of their disappointing magic performance. "I love surprises."

"Yes, sir, we sure are," Lizzie was the only one who answered as the children quickly moved to follow Zephera.

King Hiram gave a barely discernable shake of his head and softly snapped his fingers four times. It was over and done with in a split second, done so quickly and secretively no one would ever notice it. But its importance was extremely necessary. Each time Tom, Lizzie, Ned and Nell failed a magic test, he had to refresh the spell that kept his non-magical children safe from anyone else performing dangerous magic on them.

With their safety assured for the next week, the quadruplets hurriedly left the room with Zephera.

Chapter Three

"Where are we going?" asked Nell.

"I'm taking you to get your clothes measured, for the wedding and Father's birthday party," Zephera said.

"Yuck," said Tom and Ned.

"Yay!" said Lizzie and Nell. So maybe it wasn't the perfect escape for *all* four of the children, but at least they were finished with their Weekly Magic Test!

"Didn't go well in there?" Zephera sympathized, knowing the probable answer. "Cheer up, there's always next week to try it again."

"Great," Ned said sarcastically. "Thanks for the encouragement."

"Anytime," Zephera said, giving her more difficult brother a knowing smile.

"You know that we'll never be magical like the rest of you," said Tom, pointing out the obvious.

"I know," said Zephera, gently squeezing his shoulder with understanding. "But you can't blame Mom and Dad for hoping."

"Hi, Princess Zephera!" cried the same bunch of school girls the children had passed earlier. The Princess was so pretty that *of course* all the younger girls of the kingdom worshiped her.

They clustered around Zephera, admiring her dress and the ribbon tying up her blonde braids. And, *of course*, they ignored Lizzie and Nell. Except for Amaralyn, the Royal Mayor's daughter, who commented, "Test over so soon?" and giggled with her buddies.

"Is this going to take long?" Ned groaned when the girls finally pranced away.

"I promise we'll be quick," Zephera assured the quadruplets as they wound their way through the castle's maze of hallways. "I know you don't want to do it, Ned, but I thought it would be the perfect way to get you away from Mom and Dad. And the new flora-ora fabric came in –"

"Ooh – is it beautiful?" asked Lizzie, her eyes lighting up just at the thought of it. Flora-ora made the most phenomenal shining fabric that seemed to glow with a life of its own. The Royal Family had its own special patterns and colors. Certainly there would be no one else – not even that annoying Amaralyn – who would have as pretty a party dress as Lizzie and Nell.

"Ha! And it's just for us!" Nell said with glee.

"Wait until you see it," Zephera said, as she opened the door to the Royal Tailor's Shop, where the Royal Tailor and his son, Alf – Ned's nemesis – waited for them.

Zephera's wedding and King Hiram's birthday party were four weeks away, and everyone in the kingdom and the surrounding countries was looking forward to the thrilling event – everyone except King Hiram, Tom, Lizzie, Ned and Nell.

King Hiram wasn't at all happy to be turning 50 or giving his eldest daughter away in marriage.

And while Tom, Lizzie, Ned and Nell were excited for their sister's wedding, they weren't looking forward to the birthday part of the celebration because the only present their father really wanted was for them to become magical. (After them being healthy and happy, of course.)

But, obviously, there was really nothing King Hiram, Tom, Lizzie, Ned or Nell could do about any of it – getting older, Zephera getting married, *or* not being magical. So all the planning and preparations continued, regardless of their feelings.

"Why do we need new clothes?" griped Ned, grabbing a spool of thread off of the table. He started tossing it up into the air and catching it in his hand. In the corner, Ned's enemy, Alf, was watching him and saw a chance to be especially annoying by copying Ned. But Alf started tossing more and more spools into the air until 12 spools circled around his head.

"Show off," muttered Ned, and put down his lone, single, gravity-challenged spool.

"What colors can our dresses be?" enthused Nell.

"Any color you want," said Zephera to Nell. To Ned, she said, "Because it's not every day I get married and Papa turns 50, so you need new clothes."

Zephera was pledged to marry Duke Harry, a young warrior duke from Zephram who had stolen her heart away a very long time ago. She could have had her pick of princes, kings and even an Emperor, she was *that* pretty and sweet, but she'd wanted Duke Harry.

"So I asked him," she had told her startled parents, "and he said 'yes' – he was so surprised. He hadn't thought he had a chance with all those pesky princes and kings around."

King Hiram thought about Prince Persius and Emperor Mintos, the most prominent contenders for her hand, but didn't think about them anymore when he saw the bright twinkle in Zephera and Duke Harry's eyes.

The bells were rung, the date was set and the contented couple planned away.

For Zephera, that meant choosing her dress and flowers as well as the food and music. For Duke Harry, that meant taking all of his loyal soldiers to a jousting tournament just outside the Zephram border before the big day. After all, what does a groom have to do, but show up at his wedding?

"Is Duke Harry getting new clothes?" Ned asked suspiciously.

"He sure is, a bright red uniform with gold buttons and a yellow silk sash and blue pants," Zephera said. Nell and Lizzie sighed rapturously.

"Oh, he'll look so handsome!" Lizzie exclaimed.

"Yes, he will," Zephera agreed with a smile as she, too, thought about how Duke Harry would look. "That's why we're *all* going to look sharp!" She stared pointedly at her brothers.

"Don't look at me," said Tom, who had *not* been saying anything.

"Will this take long?" asked Ned again, glancing over at Alf, who started rolling his eyes at the sample sketches of the suits the boys would wear.

"I told you before, 'no' – it will only take as long as you make it take," Zephera said to the more annoying of her two brothers. "*If* you hold still – just a few minutes."

Ned grumbled and settled in to wait for his turn. He glared at Alf, who then proceeded to mumble a few quick, dastardly magical words and toss his head. Suddenly Ned found himself wearing a dress.

"Hey!" he shouted in dismay. Just a split second before everyone looked at him, his clothes switched back to normal. (Unfortunately, King Hiram's spell only protected them from danger or manipulation by the country's enemies – not from the pains of growing up.)

"Hey, what?" asked Tom.

"Nothing," Ned muttered. "I'll get you," he mouthed to Alf, who pretended to back off as if he was scared. Then he laughed and disappeared with a quick in-drawn breath and shake of his head.

"It's so romantic how you and Duke Harry found each other," Lizzie remembered, oblivious to Ned and Alf's shenanigans.

"Just like a fairy tale," said Nell.

"More like a nightmare," said Tom. "Remember how upset the other guys were? Didn't one of them want to fight a duel for you?"

"Oh, that was that nasty Prince Persius," said Nell. "Yep, he was scary –as if you'd ever marry <u>him</u>!"

"Oh, he just wanted my flora-ora," said the Princess airily.

Flora-ora was the most valuable mineral in the world, and their country, Zephram, had the largest supply around of this miracle substance. Flora-ora could be used to make almost anything: coins, tall buildings, shiny material, perfume – it could even be melted and eaten as ice cream topping! (The children could recite from memory the complete list of flora-ora uses that appeared on page 112 of the *History of Ancient Zephram*.)

"Actually, *everyone* really wanted my flora-ora when you got right down to it, no matter how handsome or clever they were," Zephera continued. "But Duke Harry – well, let's just say that we have loved each other since my third birthday party. There are plenty of other wealthy princesses out there for Prince Persius and all the others to marry."

"Not one as pretty as you," said Lizzie loyally.

"I don't think I met anyone like Duke Harry at *our* third birthday party," Nell mused.

"But, some of your boyfriends were pretty angry, Zephera," Tom pointed out again. Zephera laughed.

"What if they stole you away, and Duke Harry had to fight to get you back!" said Nell, her eyes lighting up devilishly at the thought.

"A kidnapping?" Zephera snorted. The pretty princess was also pretty down-to-earth. "I'm not that important, kiddies. Duke Harry and I are going to live happily ever after in about, oh, 28 days," she calculated. "But *first* you need some clothes."

The quadruplets allowed the Royal Tailor to take their measurements (the boys were excited to see that their outfits closely resembled the Zephram Navy's dress uniforms, with dark blue pants and a red coat, a gold belt buckle and an ornamental sword) and then they were quickly on their way back to the Royal Schoolroom, just as Zephera promised.

"Though why you're in a hurry to do more studying beats me!" said Nell to Ned as he raced ahead of them.

"Who said anything about studying?" said Ned. "I just hate that Alf. He thinks he's so great."

The quadruplets were truly relieved to see the door of their Royal Schoolroom. It felt as if they had been gone for hours when they finally got back, although it had been less than an hour. Really!

Over the years, the Royal Quadruplets' Royal Schoolroom had become their sanctuary, because they didn't have to feel so *very* different from everyone else when they were inside its four walls. But the sad fact was, they *were* different – not just because they were quadruplets (which was practically unheard of in the world), or because they were Princes and Princesses (although there were few in Zephram, there were plenty of them in other countries), but because they weren't *magical*. They were just plain, old *normal*.

They couldn't wiggle their ears and disappear or scrunch up their noses and float dinner across the Royal Dining Room Table ... or even do something as simple as pointing their fingers and turning a cow from brown to blue. They were pretty dull compared to Zephera, who could just blink and make the Royal Carpet roll up across the Royal Throne Room floor!

Now, this wouldn't be that much of a problem for most people, because there just aren't that many magical people around.

Unfortunately, though, it wasn't just their sister Zephera and their parents who had special talents. All the silly, giggly school girls, Jepson the Royal Steward, Talwin the Royal Chef – *every single person* right down to Alf, the Royal Tailor's son, was magical – *except* for Tom, Lizzie, Ned and Nell.

In fact, the Royal Quadruplets were the *first and only* documented cases of un-magical Zephramites in the thousand year history of the country. It even said so on page 40,530 of their *History of Ancient Zephram* book! How embarrassing!

In fact, no one could understand why the Royal Quadruplets weren't magical, since the Golden Ball of Zephram made *everyone* magical. Everyone!

The Golden Ball was housed in a beautiful sky-high tower at the right side of the castle (in the old palace), where it had been put when Great King Otto first discovered Zephram, over a thousand years ago.

When the Royal Quadruplets were born, their birth was celebrated all over the world because it was special that there were four of them. The kingdom was so proud of their baby princes and princesses, especially as they thought they brought four times the magic.

Then the Royal Quadruplets turned two and some things started to happen that made King Hiram and Queen Melora wonder if maybe something wasn't quite right. Or, actually, it wasn't that things started to happen, it was because they *didn't*.

Usually, a child's first sign of magic was when he or she raised up a mighty wind during a tantrum. The tiny Crown Prince and his brother and two sisters threw some magnificent temper tantrums with screaming and kicking and crying and yelling – *but no mighty wind!*

Queen Melora and King Hiram *immediately* checked the Royal Quadruplets' temperatures, which were normal, nothing out of the ordinary. At that point, they were concerned but not yet worried.

But after a few months had passed and there was no innocent fire-burping or color-changing or toy moving, it became agonizingly clear to the Royal Parents that their Royal Quadruplets lacked the expected magical powers evident in every other child in Zephram. They did nothing out of the ordinary because the Royal Quadruplets were:

ORDINARY!

Special tutors of magic from all over the world were sent for. Magicians, sorcerers, wizards, wish-granting fairies – every kind of professional came for a consultation. But even as the quadruplets got older and understood what the trouble was, and studied and practiced as hard as they could, there was *no* turning invisible, *no* turning mud into gold, *no* flying through the air, no <u>nothing</u>.

And no one could figure out why. Finally, after extensive testing of the four, the Master of Magic was forced to admit that he had done all that he could do. But King Hiram wouldn't admit defeat. He even tried scaring the quadruplets, hoping it would shock some magic out of them. He would jump out from dark corners and yell 'boo,' but while it scared the quadruplets and unnerved the castle servants, of course, it didn't scare a single bit of magic out of them.

So, a new Master of Magic took the place of the old one, and magic lessons were resumed. And then another one came. And then another one. And then another one … and all the while, the children studied their magic lessons, week after week after week. *But what was the big deal?* they wondered. Sure, it wasn't much fun being different than everyone else, and it *certainly* wasn't much fun being ordinary. But did it really matter? To King Hiram and Queen Melora, it secretly <u>did</u>. They were the only ones who remembered that page 1017 of the *History of Ancient Zephram* read that four Royal Children of Zephram would save the country and the world from a great evil.

Maybe the prophecy would take place hundreds, even thousands of years in the future. But if it meant *these* four, non-magical, Royal Children, then Zephram was in quite a pickle. For how could Zephram be saved without the powers of magic?

So King Hiram and Queen Melora kept their fingers crossed, and every week they said patiently, "Try it one more time, dears," when Tom held his breath to turn invisible and all he turned was blue; and Lizzie got dizzy when she tried spinning around to change her clothes; and Nell tried to float a book through the air but it fell to the floor instead; and Ned, well, when Ned just plain blew it worst of all, breaking his arm while trying to fly.

Because of all this, it was understandable that the quadruplets were closer than most brothers and sisters.

It wasn't much fun playing dolls with girls who could make the dolls walk and talk and suddenly appear in ornate outfits; or could whisper a 'spell' at their fingers and suddenly draw masterpieces while Lizzie and Nell's pictures looked decidedly sticklike; or riding horses and sword fighting with other boys when Ned and Tom had to actually *learn* how to do it (suffering bumps and bruises amidst the laughter); or, playing hide and seek with children who *really could* disappear from sight!

Ever since they all met years before in the Royal Nursery School, the other children couldn't help but act superior about their magic (especially Amaralyn, who thought she was so special because she could change the color of her pony to match her hair and eyes), which was *so* frustrating, because it's not like it had anything to do with skill or smarts!

All around, it was quite embarrassing to be different from everyone else in Zephram. And what made it worst of all, was that *although* they were Royal and one would hope it could be hushed up, it was *because* they were Royal that their parents hadn't been able to keep it secret. *Everyone* knew they were different!

"I hate Mondays," said Ned for the third time on that long, boring, disappointing Zephram Monday as his brother and sisters settled themselves back down in the Royal Schoolroom. "It's been hours since we ate. I'm too hungry to study. I'm going to get a flora-orasicle. Anyone want to come?"

"No, just bring us some back," said Nell. Being an obnoxious brother, Ned said, "Maybe," and left to go off to the Royal Kitchen.

Chapter Four

Once out of the Royal Schoolroom, Ned took a rambling, circuitous path to the Royal Kitchen as he was in absolutely no hurry to get back to the Royal Schoolroom. Inside the Royal Kitchen, chaos reigned as the bakers and chefs worked not just on that day's meals, but also to produce their extra Zephram Monday share.

Ned was able to grab a fistful of colorful, fruity flora-orasicles out of one of the freezers and escape with no one in the Royal Kitchen the wiser. To waste a little more time before returning to his school work, he crept back through the older passages of the original palace. Since King Hiram had declared these hallways off limits until some repairs could be made to them, he was careful to be quiet so that he would not be discovered and get into trouble.

Ned first heard the voices when he reached a great landing that opened on to a balcony overlooking the old east palace terrace. Because he knew that *he* wasn't supposed to be there, Ned was curious who *else* was there, who wasn't supposed to be there *either*.

Then he heard the voices move closer to him. He darted behind a dusty old drape that flanked the balcony opening. It was just in time, too, because a split second later two men, who he recognized as advisors to his father, appeared in the hallway. They continued walking past the spot where Ned was hidden, not noticing him.

After a moment, Ned decided to follow them so he could delay his return to the Royal Schoolroom just a little longer. Spy-fashion, he darted from shadow to shadow across the corridor, keeping a good distance between himself and his unwitting quarry.

He was beginning to get bored with the whole scheme (and besides, his flora-orasicles were starting to melt) when he heard the taller man make this interesting *and* sinister remark:

"By the end of the day, this will all be ours: the castle, the people, the flora-ora ... all of it ... when Persius comes."

The other man smiled wickedly as he replied, "Hiram is such a fool to believe the lies we tell him. I almost laughed today when he remarked that he didn't know what he would do without our help! But I held back. Our plan is too close to victory to be ruined by careless action now. We'll have plenty of time to gloat in Hiram's face once Persius gets here."

"Are the troops prepared?" asked the tall man.

"Yes. The boat arrived at dawn this morning and stayed hidden at the back of the harbor as we planned. They were unloading it a couple of hours ago. I'd say that Persius and his men will be joining us *just* in time for dinner," the shorter man estimated.

"Poor Hiram. How could he have been so stupid as to let the Princess choose her own husband? To choose Duke Harry instead of our Prince. He should have known Persius wouldn't take such humiliation."

"Or lose out on all that flora-ora!" said the other man. Both men laughed, and Ned winced. Zephera had been right when she said that the others didn't love her. They had *really* only been after her money and flora-ora.

"What about the other children?" asked the taller man. "What does Persius want to do with them?"

"What *other* children?"

"Surely you know about the Royal Quadruplets: the Crown Prince and his brother and sisters. They're quite young and they aren't magical, you know."

"Not magical?" repeated the other man, shocked. "How can that be? They're *all* magical."

"Well, *these* children aren't," said the tall man.

"Then they're not much good to anyone, are they?" said the other man, considering the news. "Persius won't want any other claims to the throne. They'll probably be disposed of. No one will miss them, I'm sure. If they're not magical, we're even sort of doing Hiram a favor!" The men laughed evilly.

Understandably, Ned didn't listen any longer. He ran for his life back the way he had come.

Chapter Five

Tom, Lizzie and Nell glanced up as the Royal Schoolroom door banged open. Ned appeared in the doorway, breathless and as pale as a ghost. The others, long settled in their studies, weren't quick to react as Ned slammed and locked the door.

"What are you doing *now*?" asked Nell with annoyance as he started dragging a bench over to block the door. "Where's my flora-orasicle?"

"We're in big trouble," Ned said, ignoring his sister and rushing over to the telescope.

"Speak for yourself," Lizzie said, as only one who is generally well behaved can. "*I* didn't steal any flora-orasicles, and I'm not ruining my dinner with junk food."

"Yes, you sure are in trouble, we *all* are," Ned said, as he wildly aimed the telescope to the left and then to the right, and then back left again. "There!" he said triumphantly.

"Hey, what are you doing? Be careful!" Tom reached out an arm to steady the telescope before Ned banged it against the window frame.

"Look, there – it's what I saw this morning in the harbor," Ned said to Tom.

Tom took a look. "Yeah, so what?"

"Well, it's not *our* army or Duke Harry," snapped Ned. "It's Prince Persius and *his* army and he's coming to marry Zephera, and 'dispose' of us, and hurt everyone."

"Why would Prince Persius do that?" asked Lizzie in a practical tone of voice. "Zephera told him 'no,' so there's no reason for him to be here."

"Unless he's coming for the wedding," said Nell, considering. "He does live in a country nearby, doesn't he?"

"You're right," agreed Lizzie. "See, Ned – that's why Prince Persius is here. If that's even him. There's not a problem."

"But maybe he didn't take it well," Nell reasoned. "He *did* seem madly in love with her. Maybe he's coming to try to get Zephera to change her mind?"

"Ha!" hooted Ned. "He wants her flora-ora."

"Ned, are you making this up?" Tom asked, suspicious of his brother.

"No, honest, this time I'm not," Ned declared. He sat down on the window seat with a loud thump. Tom looked through the telescope again and whistled.

"Well, it's an awful lot of *someone*," he said, "and you're right, those maroon flags aren't ours. What's going on – and how do *you* know about it?"

"I was on my way back with the flora-orasicles," Ned began.

"Yeah, where's mine? You didn't answer me before when I asked you," Nell interrupted, remembering again that he was to have brought her one, too.

"Sorry, I threw them away. They melted. Anyway, I was taking the long way back through the Old Palace –"

"Figures," interrupted Lizzie, ever the rule follower. "You *know* we're not supposed to be there."

"Good thing I was," Ned retorted. "When I heard voices, I hid so I wouldn't get in trouble."

"Of course you did," commented Nell.

"Do you want to hear this or not?" Ned asked.

"Sorry, I couldn't resist."

"Next thing I knew, I saw two of Dad's advisors. I heard them say Persius and his army would be here by dinner time, that Dad would be sorry, and that Persius was going to marry Zephera and take all the flora-ora. Oh, and, that Persius would probably 'dispose' of us, so there wouldn't be any other claim to the throne."

"But what about Dad and Mom?" asked Lizzie.

"I didn't hear anything about Mom and Dad, other than that Dad was going to be sorry," Ned admitted. "See if *you* hang around when you hear someone wants to 'dispose' of you."

"Ned, are you making this up?" Nell asked him, suspicious from past experience. "You know how you told us about that puppy that needed rescuing from the Baker. That he was going to bake him into a pie because he barked so much?"

"And we rescued him, but the Baker said we *stole* him," Lizzie broke in indignantly.

"And you were really just fooling, and Lizzie and I got into big trouble!" Nell finished in threatening tones.

Ned had the grace to look sheepish for just a moment. "No, this time it's real. Look out the window. I didn't make up those troops by the water, or their maroon flags."

"Who were the two men?" asked Tom, getting down to the important details.

"I don't know their names," said Ned, "but I have seen them in the Royal Throne Room with Dad a bunch of times."

"What do they look like?" asked Nell.

"One was tall and the other was short."

"And?" prompted Tom.

"And? What?" asked Ned.

"Nothing else?"

"Well, no – I was pretty far behind them. And I guess I was a little scared," he admitted reluctantly. He thought for a moment for any other helpful information he could provide. "Um, they wore blue robes."

"Every one of Dad's advisors wears a blue robe, in case you hadn't noticed," Nell said, a tad irritated.

"Would you recognize them if you saw them again?" Tom asked.

"Sure I would," said Ned. The others looked skeptical. "Really," he insisted.

"I can't believe that's all you found out," said Nell.

"Stop it," said Tom. "Now is not the time for fighting."

"If what you're saying is true, Dad should know about it," said Lizzie.

"*If* what you're saying is true," Nell pointed out.

"If Dad knows in time, our army can stop them," agreed Tom. "We'd better go tell him now, Ned. Do you girls want to come or do you want to wait here?"

"After that whole baker episode with the puppy, I have absolutely no problem with waiting here while *you* go tell Dad Ned's information," said Nell.

"Me, either," Lizzie agreed.

"We'll come straight back and let you know what happens."

As the boys left the girls chimed, "Good luck," happy to stay behind.

Walking more rapidly than they had earlier when they went for their Weekly Magic Test, Tom and Ned traveled back to the Royal Throne Room.

Although Tom spent most of their journey threatening Ned with the most dire of consequences if he wasn't telling the truth, Ned ignored him by dreaming of visions of himself as the hero who saved Zephram from invasion. Of course, now that he was with Tom, he felt invincible. And, of course, once their dad knew, he would take care of everything. Ned was certain that there was nothing in the world that he couldn't fix.

They paused outside the Royal Throne Room doors, not sure how to enter when they weren't expected. Finally, Tom just knocked. Jepson, the King's Steward, answered and looked at them blankly for a moment. He was confused because the children usually traveled in a pack of four, *not* two, and they'd ready been there today.

"May we see his Majesty?" asked Tom. Jepson was even more astonished.

"Why, I'll have to see. Just a moment," Jepson said, without his usual protocol. He looked at them again and then hustled back behind the great big wooden doors.

Tom and Ned looked at each other, the ceiling, and the floor. What should they say? Would their dad believe them? What if they were wrong? What if, surprise, surprise, Ned was wrong? (Tom would certainly kill Ned himself if he was!)

Suddenly, the Royal Thrown Room door opened and two men bowed themselves out. They looked at the princes, hesitated a second, and then walked away.

"That's them," Ned hissed, as soon as the men were out of earshot.

"Those two?" asked Tom.

"Yes," said Ned with certainty.

"I thought you couldn't describe them?"

"I *did* describe them. I said one was tall and the other one was short and they wore blue robes."

"The short one has a big scar on his face and the tall man walks with a limp and uses a cane," Tom pointed out disgustedly. "If that's all the more observant you are ... "

"Excuse me," Jepson said, poking his head out the open door. "His Majesty will see you now." He ushered them into the scene of their earlier Magic Test humiliation.

"Hello, again, boys," said King Hiram, smiling at his two sons. He waited a moment for them to speak.

They glanced at each other, silently asking who should go first: Ned as the witness or Tom as the oldest?

"What can I do for you?" asked the King helpfully a few moments later, as his sons were still silent. "Is there something you want?"

"There's something we need to tell you … uh — someone … Ned heard – uh, well, uh, who were those two men who just left?" Tom finally managed to blurt out incoherently.

"Two of my advisors," said King Hiram. "Why?"

"Do they help you a great deal?" asked Ned.

"Of course they do. A king is only as good as those who surround him. Remember that, Thomasin."

"Yes, sir," said Tom. "Do you confide in them, tell them secrets?"

"Yes, I do. One could say in some ways they know almost as much about Zephram as I do. Why all these questions?"

"We have something terribly important to tell you," Tom said. "Go ahead, Ned. It's really your news."

"Okay. Dad, I overhead those two men say that Persius had landed, and that he'd be here with his troops by dinner time to marry Zephera, and that he would take away all of the flora-ora and dispose of us," Ned said in a rush. The King frowned.

"*Those* two men?"

"Yes," said Ned.

"I'm sure there is some mistake. Those men are my spies on Persius. And I have to say that I don't like that you are making up such outrageous tales!"

"But he's not lying," Tom said, rushing to defend his brother, all the while sadly aware that Ned usually deserved the reprimand. "I saw the army landing in the harbor myself."

"You probably saw Duke Harry, if indeed you saw anyone," said the King. "I'm sure he's been missing Zephera and came back as early as he could from his tournament to surprise her. Besides, Persius is in the West, in negotiations to marry the Princess of Tolerone. As much as we love her, I don't think he's heartbroken over the loss of Zephera."

"Not Zephera, the flora-ora!" declared Ned. "He couldn't care less about Zephera."

"That's enough," said the King, getting angry. "I won't hear any more of these spiteful lies. You could be endangering two of my most trusted agents."

"But I'm not lying," said Ned.

"He's not lying," Tom said. The King looked sadly at them both.

"Nedwyn, such a tale coming from you, I could believe. But that you would involve your brother in one of your schemes is very upsetting."

"But —"

"Enough. I am going to forget that we ever had this conversation. And I hope you've learned your lesson. Nedwyn, if you have enough time on your hands to cause trouble like this, then you aren't spending enough time at your studies."

"But those two men are going to kill us," Ned boldly interrupted, managing to get out the terrible, nasty word. Unfortunately, it didn't have the desired effect. The King rolled his eyes. Tom cringed.

"Run along, I don't have time for theatrics like these," the King said.

"But," Ned tried again.

"Goodbye." The King dismissed them. Jepson held one of the heavy doors open and they had no choice but to leave.

"I can't believe you did this. I can't believe I fell for it!" Tom ranted once they got outside (and Tom rarely ranted). "I should have listened to the girls. Persius isn't going to get you – but *I* sure am! Dad's right. It's Duke Harry, you boob!"

"No, it isn't!" Ned said. "Look for yourself when we get back."

"Oh, you can bet I will!" Tom turned on his heel and stomped on back to the Royal Schoolroom, where their sisters waited. Ned slowly trailed, worried and uncertain, after him.

Chapter Six

"Well?" asked both Lizzie and Nell, when the boys opened the Royal Schoolroom door and Tom slammed it closed behind them.

"Uh, oh," said Lizzie when she saw Tom's face.

"He did it *again*," said Tom grimly.

"Of *course* he did," Nell said. "At least he didn't drag us into it this time," she said triumphantly to Lizzie. They giggled, again, at their good planning to avoid getting pulled into (and in trouble for) Ned's latest escapade.

"No, I didn't do it *again*," Ned said, going over to the telescope and looking through it. "Okay, Smart Ones – What does Duke Harry's standard look like?" he asked.

"Green with yellow eagles," said Nell.

"No, that's that cute Count Franco's flag," said Lizzie.

"Oh, you're right," agreed Nell.

"I'm pretty sure Duke Harry's is maroon with blue unicorns and gold stars," said Lizzie. "Why?"

"Here's why – Tom, what do *you* see?"

Tom groaned. He hesitated for a moment and then curiosity got a hold of him. He walked over to Ned and took one more look through the telescope.

"Well?" asked Ned triumphantly. "What do *those* flags look like?"

"Maroon with a green serpent. Oh, make that serpents. And they're heading toward the castle. Okay, you're right, Ned," Tom admitted reluctantly. "But *now* what do we do?"

"Wait, let me see," cried Nell as she rushed over to look through the telescope herself. "Uh, oh, you're right."

"What did Dad say when you told him?" asked Lizzie.

"He didn't believe us, of course. He says the two men are his spies on Persius and that he trusts them completely. He also thinks the troops are Duke Harry's, and that he has come back early to surprise Zephera."

"Forget for a minute that Ned started this whole thing. Why would *you* lie about something like that?" asked Nell.

"Of course, *I* wouldn't," said Tom, "but Ned would." Lizzie and Nell frowned at their brother.

"I *didn't* lie. And the proof's right out there."

"Okay, this time you didn't lie. I actually wish you had," Tom said. "Those troops out there are definitely not Duke Harry's. So someone is marching toward the castle right now – and that can't be good."

"Well, then we'll just have to go tell Dad," said Lizzie.

"Right – be my guest," said Ned. "Remember? It didn't go so well just now!"

"I don't know if we'd even be able to get in to see him again," admitted Tom. "He was kind of annoyed about the whole thing."

"Well, if there really is someone with a flag with snakes on it – ugh – skulking towards us, I'm not going to wait around to be disposed of," said Lizzie in practical tones. "Let's go get some help."

"That's just what I was thinking," said Nell, coming over to sit down beside Lizzie.

"What?" sputtered Ned. "Go get help? Just like that? Good idea," he added sarcastically.

"You want to hang out *here* and wait around for the end?" asked Lizzie.

"No, but just what kind of help do you think you're going to find?" asked Ned.

"Why, we can go get Duke Harry, you great big oaf, since *he's* not the army that's here," said Nell.

"Besides, Duke Harry will be *very* upset if Zephera gets herself married to Prince Persius," said Lizzie.

"That's a stupid –"

"That's a great idea," said Tom. "We could get there and back pretty quickly." He turned to look at the map hanging on the Royal Schoolroom wall and placed his finger on the spot, just outside of Zephram, where Duke Harry and his troops were attending (and hopefully winning) their pre-wedding tournament.

"You think it could work?" Ned asked, annoyed he hadn't thought of it himself.

"Unless we go and get him, by the time he comes for the wedding it will be too late," said Nell.

"Plus, he'd be walking into a trap," said Tom. "I think it's our only chance. We wouldn't have to go that far, and it's in the opposite direction of the harbor where *they're* coming from," he said, still looking at the map. "Duke Harry will be heading back. We'll just have to figure out where we'll run into him."

"We'll need to pack," said Lizzie, ever practical.

"Okay, let's think this through," Tom said. The four settled down around the table which was piled high with their homework. The boys pushed the heavy *History of Ancient Zephram* out of their way.

"I don't think we can leave just yet," Tom said, chewing his lip as he thought.

"Why not?" asked Nell.

"I think we need to be completely sure before we go that it *isn't* Duke Harry with a surprise for Zephera. We'd get in big trouble if it was. Mom and Dad would think we'd run away from home."

That was smart of Tom, because that's something most Moms and Dads would be mad about, too. "I think we'll need to do it like this," he continued, dropping his voice to a whisper. Nell, Ned and Lizzie listened carefully and added some suggestions, and between the four of them they managed to work out their rescue mission, just in case they really did end up needing one for the kingdom.

~Z~

Chapter Seven

At 6:45 that evening, the Royal Quadruplets settled themselves to wait for the invasion of Zephram. They hid in a place within the castle that only Ned and the Royal Bat Keeper knew about.

Tom, Lizzie, Ned and Nell were right smack in the center of the vast Royal Dining Hall, but far *above* it, not in it. They were actually looking down from the balcony located around the mounting of the great chandelier.

The outer windows of this towered portion allowed plenty of fresh air (and bats) into the Royal Dining Hall. (Thank goodness the bats were out hunting for their dinner at the moment!)

The chandelier was lit by a flick of the Royal Electrician's wrist from way down below, so no one would have any reason to be up here where the children sat. The only way to get up here if anyone *really* wanted to (other than with magic), was to go through the hidden passage the children had used, which Ned had discovered years ago. So the four felt relatively sure that they would not be discovered up in their perch as they waited to find out if anything was going to happen.

As they carefully leaned over the opening into the tower's shaft, they could see the country's nobles entering the room, the musicians setting up, and the servants hustling around. Beside them were their knapsacks which they had spent the last hour filling up with:

- Food (especially flora-ora butter!)
- Blankets and clothing
- Bandages and flora-ora cream
- A little knife to make sandwiches
- Tom's astrolabe and compass
- A map and water bottles

(Ned had been in charge of the food because he was the most skilled at slipping in and out of the Royal Kitchen.) They were all packed and ready, *if* they ended up having to go.

"Their Royal Highnesses," they suddenly heard Jepson announce from way down below. The four exchanged glances. Lizzie crossed her fingers and Tom gritted his teeth. Surely, any minute they would know if there was going to be a problem?

The crowd sank obediently to honor King Hiram and Queen Melora, as they made their Royal Way to the head of the great Royal Dining Table.

Princess Zephera was announced next, and she followed her parents to her seat at the table, a sparkling pretty picture of a princess in her ice-blue flora-ora beaded dress. (The quadruplets weren't missed. They weren't normally part of the procession because they would usually be eating quietly in their own quarters, too young to be invited to a grown-up dinner.) Their parents sat down, after which all of the guests sat down, and everyone started talking. It seemed like a normal Royal Dinner, with nothing out of the ordinary.

The quadruplets exchanged glances.

Was anything going to happen?

When would it happen?

How would it happen?

How much longer?

Would their plan work?

All of a sudden, the ornate, heavy doors broke open, and evil Prince Persius marched arrogantly into the Royal Dining Hall.

"Ah, King Hiram! So nice of you to hold dinner for me," he exclaimed, as men-at-arms poured in behind him and took aggressive stances by King Hiram's own personal guard. Sounds of chaos from the outer halls echoed into the room.

"Uh, oh!"

"Oh, dear!"

"Oh, no!"

"I told you so!"

Hidden way up in the tower, three of the four looked at each other with dread, while Ned looked smug at his vindication.

"Prince Persius, what is going on? What is the meaning of this?" demanded King Hiram as the horrible scene unfolded beneath the children.

"It's *King* Persius to you, Hiram," Prince Persius said. "I'm here today to take over your country, marry your daughter and take your flora-ora. And, after I do all that, I believe that makes me *King* of Zephram. So, yes, it's *King* Persius to you."

"Take us over? Why, you *can't* take us over!" blustered King Hiram. "We're – we're –"

"Magical?" Prince Persius interrupted helpfully. "HA, HA, HA, HA, HA!" he laughed. It wasn't a nice laugh. "Not anymore."

He gestured, and one of his guards came over carrying something wrapped in a thick blanket.

"What do we have here?" Prince Persius teased. "Let's take a look, shall we?" He carefully pulled the blanket away and the noble citizens of Zephram gasped in collective horror at what was revealed:

It was the magic GOLDEN BALL! The Golden Ball that the *History of Ancient Zephram* said, on page 25, made all of the people of Zephram (all *except* for the Royal Quadruplets) magical.

King Hiram blinked hard and pointed his finger at Prince Persius, to make him and all his men go away, or disappear, or roll up in the rug, or anything. But nothing happened. King Hiram turned pale. His advisors looked sick.

THE MAGIC HAD STOPPED WORKING!

"Return the Golden Ball to me at once!" demanded King Hiram, managing to muster his deep kingly voice, despite the situation.

"Oh, but you see, I can't," said Prince Persius, not looking at all sorry. "Because if I gave it back to you, you'd get all your magic back. I wouldn't be able to take over the country, marry Zephera and have all the flora-ora. So I can't. So sorry!"

"By the way," he continued quite casually, "you really *should* have a guard on your little *magic ball*, Hiram. Why, *anyone* could have just gone up and taken it. Oops, that's right – that's just what *I* did."

"Everyone is happy here in Zephram," said King Hiram. "No one has ever needed to steal it."

"Well, *I* needed to steal it," said Persius, "and since I did, it looks like now *I'll* be the happy one here in Zephram."

"What do you really want, Persius?"

"I *told* you: I want to take over the country, marry Zephera and have all your lovely flora-ora." He waited a moment. "Or, I guess you could just give me three billion florites, whichever is easier for you. I don't really need two kingdoms, especially if you pay me every year. Two kingdoms would just be a hassle to run."

He considered this new deal. "Oh, but, I guess I'd still want to be called King, and I'd still make Zephera my wife, whatever you decide. Either way, it sounds like a win win situation for me. But you know what's *really* funny?" he paused for a dramatic effect. "That magic ball of yours doesn't even make *me* magic. All it did was turn off *your* magic when I grabbed it. HA, HA, HA, HA, HA! So it looks like your *magic* is pretty overrated, don't you think, Hiram? What do you think, Darling?" he turned to Zephera.

"Don't call me 'Darling.' And, I will NOT marry you," said the Princess, stamping her foot and not the least bit afraid. "I told you NO already. I am marrying my true love, Duke Harry."

"Blah, blah, blah, I can't hear you, Darling," said Prince Persius, covering his ears with his hands, just as children do to annoy a brother or sister. "You'll marry me as soon as it can be arranged."

"We'll see about that," Zephera said to him with a dangerous scowl.

"So, three billion florites, or your kingdom. It's your choice, Hiram. What will it be?" Prince Persius asked, raising the total of the ransom.

"You are *not* marrying Zephera!" cried Queen Melora.

'No!" agreed King Hiram. "And I don't have three billion florites to give you. Why, it would take a month of Zephram Mondays to raise money like that!"

"Hiram, what a spectacular idea!" exclaimed Prince Persius. "*Thank* you for thinking of it for me. Today still being Monday, you can start working tonight!" He turned to the two advisors Ned had seen earlier. "Aren't these Zephram Mondays just the best idea?"

"But my subjects, all of us, need our magic to get our work done," pointed out King Hiram.

"And I need your reserves of flora-ora. Or, of course, 30 billion florites. Did I say three billion before? Silly me, I meant 30 billion. So, it's flora-ora or 30 billion florites, whichever you care to give me. Looks like you'll just have to try working without magic. I hope it's not too hard for you."

Prince Persius leaned over to confer with the two evil advisors the boys had seen earlier.

"That's them," Ned whispered to the girls. Persius turned back to King Hiram.

"Listen, Hiram, being a good fellow and all, I'll give you tonight to think it over in the dungeon. It's the least I can do. I'll check in with you tomorrow morning. But for the rest of you, dinner's over! You can get right to work <u>now</u>! HA, HA, HA, HA, HA!"

Several of his guards came to take King Hiram and Queen Melora to the dungeon.

"Zephera, you can stay here with me, Darling."

"Never!" cried the Princess.

"Okay, then suit yourself," said Prince Persius unconcernedly. Princess Zephera ran after her parents. Immediately, the nobles, who had been sitting at the tables watching in horror as the invasion unfolded, were rounded up by the guards and escorted off to continue the Zephram Monday work they thought they had finished before dinner.

The two evil advisors remained in the Royal Dining Room.

"*Well* done," crowed Prince Persius. "I couldn't be more pleased with how this whole invasion went. And a Month of Zephram Mondays' worth of ransom! Inspired. I don't know why I waited so long to try this. It was so easy! Is everything and everyone secure?"

"Yes, all but those quadruplets. The Crown Prince, and his brother and sisters. They weren't in the Royal Schoolroom when the guards looked there."

"Find them," said Prince Persius, in a deadly tone, all joking over with.

"Yes, Sir," said Nordon and Fruston (for those were their names).

"Time to go," said Tom from their hiding place way up above the fray. The four children gathered up their belongings and left.

Chapter Eight

The castle may have had all its exits and entrances closed and guarded by enemy soldiers, but that didn't stop the four inquisitive youngsters from getting out (especially Ned, who knew every nook and cranny of the castle).

Tom, Lizzie and Nell followed closely behind Ned as he took them through dusty hidden hallways, and up and down rickety stairs, until at last they came to a long forgotten passage way he told them they would be able to use to take them to the Royal Stables.

"You're sure this is the only way out?" Nell asked with dread, looking at the tunnel's tiny opening that was hidden behind the ancient Royal Furnace in the unused Old Palace. The opening was just about as high as their hips, and it was really, really dark inside.

"Yes," said Ned. "Or we could use the Front Gate, if you'd rather."

"Ha, ha," said Nell. "You're so funny."

"Do you think we'll be able to fit in there with our knapsacks?" Lizzie asked, looking over her shoulder at her over-stuffed bag.

"I think we'll have to crawl," Tom said. They could hear the faint sounds of the soldiers' pounding footsteps, far enough away for the moment, but they certainly didn't want to wait for them to sound as if they were coming any nearer.

"I'll go first," Ned volunteered. He crouched down at the entrance to pull a few stringy, dusty strands aside and bravely crawled into the dark hole. It was a tight fit, but he made it.

With grimaces, the girls got down on their hands and knees to crawl after Ned, and Tom brought up the rear after he squeezed around in the tight space to pull the cobwebs back across the opening.

Other than getting dirty and dealing with what the girls called the 'yuck factor,' the children arrived safely at the other end of the tunnel. Thankfully, they found it opened up and they were able to stand in the bigger space. In the ceiling overhead there was a trap door.

"So will we end up in a stall when we open the door?" asked Lizzie as they stood on their tiptoes to push and strain at the trap door.

"Yes," grunted Ned. "I think it's Malowen's stall." If true, that could be unfortunate. Malowen was King Hiram's trusty charger and he didn't like the children. But what choice did they have?

"Do you think he's standing on top of the door?" grunted Tom as they continued to push. Either Malowen must have been elsewhere in the stall or the door was just stuck from never being used, because the side that Nell was pushing against suddenly broke free.

"Everyone *push*," said Tom at that encouraging sign, and they were able to open the door with their extreme renewed effort.

Ned gave his knapsack to Lizzie to hold, and grabbed the door frame with his hands to pull himself up into the stall.

"The coast is clear," he called down to the others, after looking around the small area. "Malowen's in the corner. Watch out for the poop."

Nell was the next one to appear, easily pulling herself up through the hole. Malowen nickered softly but he must have understood something was wrong, because he let them come in without charging them or stamping his hooves.

"Geez, how much *do* you poop, Malowen?" Nell asked, carefully picking her way around. Ned helped Lizzie next and then Tom pulled himself up. The boys lowered the door back into place.

"Let's cover it with some straw," Tom suggested. Ned grabbed a pitchfork to pull some over while Nell moved some with her feet.

"So we just go out the Royal Stable door?" Lizzie asked. She had bravely approached Malowen and was gently stroking his long nose.

"Watch he doesn't bite your hand," said Nell.

"Oh, he's just a big baby," said Lizzie.

"I think we should go out this way," Ned said, pointing to a small doorway at the back of the stall through which the Royal Stable Hands swept all the poop.

"Yuck," said Nell.

"Are you sure we can't just go out the real door?" Lizzie asked.

"No way!" exclaimed Ned, putting down the pitchfork. "It's brilliant, if I say so myself. No one is going to look for us in the poop."

"*You* are a poop," declared Nell.

"I don't think we have much of a choice," said Tom. He walked over to the hatch and pushed it open.

"There's not a lot," he said after he looked out. "You just need to sort of leap way over to the right."

"I wish we could take our horses," Lizzie sighed.

"I wish we could, too, but they'll be hard to take through the Royal Forest since we won't be on the road. I don't want them to get hurt."

"You're right. I hadn't thought of that."

"Well, let's get it over with," said Nell, walking over to the hatch. "You first," she said, and gave Ned a big shove.

"Cleared it," they heard him hiss triumphantly in a loud whisper.

"Here goes," Nell said, and the three made the leap across the pile of manure to become free: free of the Royal Stables, the walled castle grounds, and, most importantly, *Prince Persius*.

The Royal Quadruplets fled into the darkness of the night and across the wide stretch of land that separated the castle from the Royal Forest. Once they were safely in the forest and away from Prince Persius and the dinner invasion and takeover, their heartbeats slowed down, and they were less afraid (actually Ned thought it was a fun adventure).

It was all great to plan to leave the castle and save the country, but once they were actually outside, they started to realize the *enormity* of what had just happened inside to their parents, their sister, the Zephram citizens – and the *enormity* of the rescue mission they had set for themselves.

Plus …

"I'm hungry. We missed dinner, you know," Ned reminded his brother and sisters as they hustled through the trees.

"How can you think of eating *now*?" hissed Nell, stumbling a little as her eyes got used to the darkness.

"Eating makes me think better," said Ned.

"I guess here's as good a place as any to stop for a moment," Tom said, and the others gratefully plopped down onto the ground. They were a scant 500 feet from the castle wall, but they were hidden from view by a heavy curtain of tree branches.

From the outside, looking back at the city, no one would ever guess that a major revolution was taking place inside. In fact, a revolution had never happened in the thousand year history of Zephram!

Zephram had been a peaceful and prosperous country from the moment it was discovered by Great King Otto. King Otto was King Hiram's great – well, he was a *really* great-grandfather from way back.

When King Otto was young man and just *Prince* Otto, he needed a country of his own because his older brother was already the king of their country, Golara. So, the Wizard of the castle (who was also Prince Otto's godfather) gave him a beautiful sphere, a golden ball just about the size of a basketball to take on his travels as he looked for a place to be a king.

The Wizard told Prince Otto that when the sphere lit up, Prince Otto would have found his *own* country, and he would be the king of it.

The Prince traveled far and wide, and he had a lot of great adventures. He fought dragons and ogres, and he befriended fairies. He traveled through Winter and Spring, Summer and Fall, and back through Winter into Spring again, all the while taking special care of his golden ball. Finally, he was stopped in his travels because a great blue ocean was in front of him, and he couldn't go any farther without a boat or at least a raft, and he didn't have either of those things with him.

He started looking in the forest he had just passed through for trees and tree limbs that he might be able to use to build a raft, when suddenly the golden ball started vibrating and humming. Then, it lit up brilliantly, glowing with a light Prince Otto had never seen before.

When he looked around, Prince Otto was excited to realize he had found a huge deposit of flora-ora. Back in his old country, they didn't have any flora-ora and they had to pay a lot of money to buy it from other countries.

His first thought was that he could use the flora-ora to make a raft. Then he realized that he could actually use it to build an entire ship. And then he realized he could feed his horses with it. In fact, he then realized there was *so much* he could do with the flora-ora that, in his excitement, he lost count of its uses.

And then, he remembered the prophecy that his godfather, the Wizard, had made: that when the Ball lit up, he would have found his own country. Prince Otto was home!

Needless to say, Prince Otto didn't have to build a raft or go any further. What he built instead was a huge, walled city, right there by the ocean and the flora-ora. The city and seaport became his new country, Zephram, and he became *King* Otto of a beautiful and prosperous country.

But that wasn't all that happened. King Otto, and all of his friends who came to live with him in the new country of Zephram, woke up one morning to suddenly find that *they* had *magical* powers. Somehow, the combination of the Golden Ball and the flora-ora brought out the little bit of magic that was deep inside each one of them, and all the citizens of Zephram became *magical*.

(That's when, out of gratitude, King Otto enacted the very first Zephram Monday to make sure that *all* of his subjects would *always* benefit from the country's prosperity.)

Those wonderful magical powers continued uninterrupted through the centuries, until the birth of the <u>very first cases</u> of non-magical Zephram subjects, the ordinary Royal Quadruplets (who apparently didn't have even the *tiniest* bit of magic, not even buried deep inside of them).

And now those four, non-magical children sat hidden in the Royal Forest, outside *their* Royal City Walls, having made it safely through the first part of their mission. They could feel the weight of the responsibility to save their kingdom from evil Prince Persius resting firmly on their young shoulders.

"Anyone want a sandwich?" Ned asked. Best to worry about first things first.

Chapter Nine

Ned pulled a flora-ora butter and jelly sandwich out of his knapsack. He carefully unwrapped it, stashed the trash paper back into his bag, and started eating. After a moment, the others got out their sandwiches, too.

"That's better," Ned said presently. "I was getting too hungry to think."

"Oh, so you can't think because you're hungry?" teased Nell. "*That's* why?"

Ned made a face at her but didn't say anything, for which Tom was glad because it was really too soon to have to deal with them fighting.

"Okay, Plan A, escaping from the castle, is done. Now we have to make it to the Rock Field before dawn," he said. "We really can't stop here for long. There's a lot of forest to get through and Persius's troops are probably going to be following us any minute.

"Once we get past the Rock Field we shouldn't have to worry about them," Tom continued. "Those boulders are so hard to get over, I don't think they could do it without breaking their necks."

"I bet when they see what we do to the rocks they'll think we're dead anyway," Nell said with glee.

"Don't say that!" Lizzie cried, shuddering.

"Sorry."

"But it's true," Ned pointed out. "If they think we're uh – *gone*," he substituted with a look at Lizzie, "they'll go back to the castle and tell Prince Persius. Without them following us, it'll make it easier to go get Duke Harry."

"Hey, what do you guys think of this idea?" Tom asked suddenly. "If we walked *this* way it would take us straight to the Rock Field," he said, looking at his compass and then pointing ahead, "but I don't think we want to make too easy for them to follow us, do we?"

"No, or catch up to us until we get there in the morning," agreed Ned.

"So, how about if we went west first, and then doubled back and looped past the Bog Marsh? Just for some fun," Tom said, explaining his change to the plan.

"Some stinky fun," said Lizzie, getting into the spirit of it, and the four chuckled gleefully, imagining how annoyed Persius's men were going to be after spending all night looking for the quadruplets.

"So, I guess we don't get to sleep tonight?" asked Nell, after they got up and started walking in the new direction.

"No," said Tom, "not until we get *past* the Rock Field." He started breaking tree limbs and stepping on the grasses. "Ned, can you rip some of those leaves above you so they can see by the markings that we went this way?"

"After we sleep, maybe we could take a little break and practice the magic we're giving Dad for his birthday present," said Lizzie, scattering some stones with the toe of her shoe. "Otherwise, I'm afraid we won't be ready to do it for him when we get back."

The other three actually stopped in their tracks to look at her in amazement.

"Won't be ready?!?" Nell cried in disbelief. Ned snorted.

"Lizzie," Tom asked, exasperated, "do you really, *seriously* believe that we will *ever* be magical?"

"Well, I think if we just keep trying –"

"Lizzie, you may not have tried very hard but I sure have," said Ned. "Remember that hard white thing I had on my arm for two months called a cast? I don't want another one. Magic hurts when it doesn't work!"

"And no matter how many times I twirl around, my clothes don't change. I just get dizzy and fall over, in case you hadn't noticed," said Nell. "And, I don't see you having much success with that whole turning water into soda pop thing, either."

"The only way we've ever been able to make something disappear is to put it away in a drawer, and that doesn't count," Tom pointed out. "Lizzie, we can't try any harder. We just *aren't* magical."

"Okay, but if it's not magic, what do we get Dad for his birthday?" Lizzie asked stubbornly.

"Don't you think we're a little busy with this whole invasion and rescue mission thing?" Ned asked.

"I think we should worry about Dad's present later. We've got a month until his birthday, you know," Nell comforted her sister. "I'm sure we'll think of something."

Suddenly they could hear a commotion in the distance behind them: men's rough voices and neighing horses and thundering hooves.

"It sounds like they've finally left the castle to find us. Let's keep moving," Tom urged, and they quickened their steps through the night, stumbling in the dark on tree roots and rocks.

As they had planned, the quadruplets led Prince Persius's unsuspecting men back and forth *and* back and forth through the Royal Forest. Because it was dark and they were unfamiliar with the Royal Forest, the soldiers didn't catch on at all that they were being led astray. Not until they stepped right smack into the Bog Marsh.

Not only did they *not* know there was a Bog Marsh in the Royal Forest, it became clear they obviously didn't know *anything* about Bog Marshes, just as the children had hoped.

The Bog Marsh looked just like the rest of the Royal Forest floor because it was hidden underneath the leaves and rubble. But as soon as the men stepped onto it, they where horrified to find themselves sinking knee deep into a thick, sticky, gluey mess that they had no idea was there *or* what it was.

Immediately, their boots stuck and could only be pulled out with great effort. Unfortunately, once the boot moved, it opened up great whiffs of sulfur-smelling air (like rotten eggs or garbage) that practically knocked them over because the stench was so awful.

Now, the Bog Marsh was only two feet deep, so the quadruplets knew that the men wouldn't be hurt (as much as they may have wanted them to be). And the terrible smell was just gross, not poisonous. But the evil soldiers didn't know either of those things (hee, hee), and dealing with the bog kept the soldiers scared and busy for a good fifteen or twenty minutes, giving the children enough time to get to the Rock Field and set up their next plan.

Holding their breath and trying not to laugh, they crept away as quietly and quickly as possible, while the bad men were shouting with fright and annoyance from the stinky distraction.

Finally, just as dawn was breaking, the tired children reached the Rock Field, pleased to be well ahead of Persius's men.

"Okay, so far, so good," Tom said. They were exhausted from hiking all night. "We can rest soon," Tom assured his sisters, who dragged behind the boys.

"Time for Plan B?" Ned asked.

"Time for Plan B," Tom said, and the two boys got a wicked gleam in their eyes as they started pulling things out of their knapsacks.

As far as the eye could see, what looked like a vast gray sea stretched away from the quadruplets. But it wasn't a sea of water, it was a sea of boulders, deposited there by an ancient glacier, tens of thousands of years ago.

Of course, crossing the Rock Field wasn't easy. The best way to cross over was with magic, to blink one's self to the other side. But, of course, the quadruplets weren't magical. So they always had to do it the way they did everything else: the old fashioned way, which usually meant the hard way. In this case, it meant they had to climb.

There were plenty of easier routes the children could have taken to reach Duke Harry. But when they were planning their escape, they realized it would be practically impossible to reach Duke Harry and *his* men if evil, armed men on horseback were chasing *after* them.

Tom felt they had to do something that would convince Persius's men they could abandon their search. That way, the quadruplets could continue *their* rescue mission without the enemy in hot pursuit.

The problem with many of the other, easier routes the children had considered, was that there was no good way to make sure they permanently 'ditched' the men. Taking advantage of the Rock Field was their best option.

The children settled down to work, assembling the extra pieces of clothing they'd packed: a shoe, a shirt, a slipper, a little crown, a tunic, a pair of pants, a skirt, a jacket, a vest, a muff. They'd brought just a piece or so to represent each child by their Prince and Princess appearance.

"I've always hated this skirt," Nell said as she gritted her teeth and started ripping it. Lizzie took the slipper and rubbed its pretty satin toe in the dirt while Ned stomped on the crown, bending it out of shape.

Tom had just as much fun as his brother and sisters did, but he watched the sky and listened carefully while he was destroying his jacket.

"Okay, let's put the clothes out," he said, when they felt enough damage had been done. After checking to make sure they were still alone, Tom and Ned carefully climbed onto the Rock Field and scattered the clothing on top of the boulders.

"It's time for the flora-ora noodle sauce!" Ned said excitedly.

"Stay there, we'll bring it out to you," Nell said. The girls took the containers of red-colored sauce out of their knapsacks and slowly worked their way out to join their brothers on the boulders.

There, the children found that as much fun as it had been ruining their Prince and Princess clothing, it was *nothing* compared to the fun they had squirting flora-ora noodle sauce all over the clothing and boulders!

After looking over the carefully-staged scene and giving it one last squirt of sauce, the quadruplets settled back into the trees at the edge of the Royal Forest to wait for dawn and for Prince Persius's men to catch up to them.

Chapter Ten

The quadruplets didn't have very long to wait to begin the next stage of Plan B.

Every single morning at precisely 15 minutes after dawn, the Wild Hydrox of Rock Field rose up out of her nest in the surrounding treetops and swooped over the boulders, screeching so loudly that she usually woke up the countryside.

It was an eerie, frightening sound, and she was an eerie, <u>huge</u>, frightening bird. In order for Plan B to work, the quadruplets were hoping that, just like the Bog Marsh, Persius's men didn't know about the Wild Hydrox. Hopefully, the men would be surprised *and* terrified when they saw her *and* the quadruplets' little display.

After a few minutes, the quadruplets could hear Persius's men working their way through the trees. The men sounded extremely annoyed at how the children had led them around and around and around. Plus, they were scared of what Persius would say and do to them, if they had to tell him they lost the Royal Children.

"Hope he puts them in the dungeon, too," whispered Nell.

"Or worse," Ned added.

Just at that moment, the Wild Hydrox appeared, beating her mighty wings, stirring the air for hundreds of yards around as she took off from her nest, shrieking her scary sound.

That was the cue for the four children to start shrieking themselves: shrieking, shrieking, shrieking and shrieking. Finally, they stopped shrieking, and dove back under the tree cover at the edge of the field.

Persius's men burst through the trees. In front of them all they could see were the Royal Quadruplets' clothes – stained, torn and scattered as if the children had been attacked. Above them the men could see the horribly ugly Wild Hydrox, slowly sweeping across the sky, her large shadow darkening the Rock Field. She still cried her terrible cry.

What did the men think when they saw and heard all the evidence – the screams, the scattered red-stained clothing, the huge ugliness of the bird? That the Royal Children had met their end, attacked and eaten by the Wild Hydrox!

Suddenly, the Wild Hydrox turned and started her flight back to her nest, shrieking all the way. The men took one look at the bird flying back toward them, and took off back into the Royal Forest as fast as they could.

The funniest part of Plan B was that the Wild Hydrox had absolutely no idea what had just happened. No idea at all. She circled her nest, carefully landed, shrieked her last shriek and settled down for a breakfast of leaves and twigs. She didn't even eat meat (let alone Royal, although un-magical, Children)!

"It worked!" Ned whispered, and made as if to stand up.

"Wait," Tom cautioned, pulling him back down. Sure enough, a couple of minutes later, the men ventured back into the open.

"Go grab the clothes," one man, who looked important, said to the soldier next to him.

"But what if it gets me, too?" asked the other man, looking up at the sky.

"*Persius* will get you if you don't get the clothes to prove those brats are dead," said the important looking man. Obviously the thought of Persius was even more frightening than the Wild Hydrox, because the man crept out onto the boulders to retrieve the children's stuff. A few minutes later, the soldiers left.

Needless to say, the children were delighted that their plan worked. But they were also very, very tired. They waited about 15 minutes to make sure that the men were really not coming back, and then they settled into a natural cavern, made by the rocks at the edge of the Rock Field, to take an overdue nap.

Chapter Eleven

The quadruplets slept soundly until lunch time, when their growling stomachs woke them up. It sure was hard, hungry, exhausting work to save their country!

"*Now* what do we do? Are we going to get going soon?" asked Nell, as they munched on their flora-ora butter and jelly sandwiches and drank water from the water bottles they had brought along. They had packed enough supplies to have 10 sandwiches each because that was all they had room for in their knapsacks, but they were already down to eight. At this rate, they would soon be eating tree branches!

"No, I think we'll have to wait until dusk before we can start across the Rock Field," Tom said, looking out at the boulders sparkling in the sunlight.

Ned agreed. "We're too easy to see out there now. I still can't believe they fell for our trick. Plan B was awesome!" he continued, remembering their early morning's activity.

"But won't it be hard for *us* to see if we cross the Rock Field later?" asked Nell.

"Not if we have some little lights to help us," Tom said.

"And where are *we* going to get those?" asked Lizzie logically. Magical Zephramites didn't have need for little lights when they could just magically make something light up, so there hadn't been anything for the quadruplets to pack.

"I'm thinking we can capture lightning bugs at dusk, and put them in our water bottles until we cross the field."

"That's a great idea," said Nell. "I love catching lightning bugs.

"But, Tom, we can't throw away our water," Lizzie said, concerned.

"We can refill our bottles at the edge of the field. There's a river right *here*, I think, if I am reading this map correctly," he said, referring to the map he had spread out in front of them.

"When do you think we can reach Duke Harry?" asked Ned, looking down at the map.

"Maybe two or three days if we walk fast," Tom speculated. "We should meet them right about *here*."

"So we could be back home by the beginning of next week if all goes well," Ned said, considering the time frame and measuring distances with his fingers.

"*If* all goes well," agreed Tom.

"What do you think Mom and Dad are doing right now?" asked Lizzie.

The children were suddenly sad.

"Probably having lunch like we are," Tom said, trying to cheer them up. 'I'm sure they're fine."

"But Prince Persius took them to the dungeon," Lizzie said.

"But our dungeons aren't too scary," Ned said, because he, of course, had checked them out many times while exploring the castle. "I mean, they're dark. And cold. But there aren't too many rats — well, they've got cots and blankets," he continued, seeing Lizzie's look of horror.

"And I'm sure there are curtains at the windows," Nell said, trying to cheer Lizzie up.

"No, I didn't see any windows," Ned said. Nell punched him in the arm, and he shut up.

"I know we're worried about Mom and Dad. But all we can do right now is get to Duke Harry, and bring him and his army home as soon as possible. That's the best way we can help Mom and Dad, and Zephera too." Tom said stoutly. "It's going to be another long night, so why don't we try to get a little more sleep."

"Okay," Lizzie agreed, "but do you think they miss us?"

"Lizzie," the other three groaned.

"Okay, okay," she said.

"Remember, we really haven't been gone very long," Nell comforted her with a quick hug, and they settled in for a post flora-ora butter and jelly nap.

At dusk, the children packed up their meager belongings in their knapsacks and prepared to leave their makeshift home. As if on cue, the lightning bugs appeared with their gently sparkling lights.

The four took last drinks from their water bottles and emptied them. For a few moments, they forgot their troubles as they chased the lightning bugs, and captured as many as they could, putting them in the water bottles. They then carefully covered the openings with cotton material Tom had tucked away while ripping clothes at the Rock Field, so the lightning bugs were able to breathe.

With their way lit by the flickering lightning bugs, the quadruplets carefully stepped across the Rock Field without any mishaps. By the time they were safely across, the moon was high in the night sky. They could hear water rushing nearby.

"Hey, there *is* water. You were right," Ned said, as they saw the river Tom had identified earlier on the map.

Lizzie stopped to loosen the tie from around her water bottle and let her lightning bugs go.

"Thanks for your help," she called as they flew off. The others quickly emptied their bottles of the lightning bugs, too.

As they walked through the trees to a clearing, they came upon the river. The water stretched like ink in the darkness, mirroring the starry sky and the path of the moon, while little floating edges of white foam appeared here and there in the current.

Unfortunately, no helpful bridge stretched across the river. No helpful rowboat waited for them, either.

"Hum," Tom said, surveying their options, of which there appeared to be none.

"Should we swim?" asked Ned.

"I don't think it would be safe to swim in the dark now, but I don't think we can wait until morning when it's light, either."

"Hum," agreed Lizzie.

"You know what," Nell said, as an idea dawned. "I can climb up there and get that vine," she said. 'Up there' where Nell pointed was a vine-draped branch a good 15 to 20 feet up an old water oak tree.

"And we could use the vine to tie together some logs and maybe make a raft," Tom continued her thoughts.

Nell laid her bottle, knapsack and her sweater on the ground.

"You'll need this," Lizzie said, handing her a dull knife they used to spread the flora-ora butter. "But are you sure you want to do this?"

"Piece of cake," Nell, the natural gymnast, said, and without another thought, started her climb up the tree. In the meantime, Tom and Ned started pulling some broken tree limbs closer together into a pile to see just what they had to work with.

"Are you being careful?" Lizzie asked, peering up into the branches.

Nell didn't bother answering her worried sister. Within moments, she had reached the vine. With her great balance and sure-footedness, she walked quickly across the branch and reached above her head to yank at the vine. She sawed through the tough fibers with the little knife to separate the vine from where it wrapped around itself.

"Heads up," she called, letting yards of the vine drop below. "Do you want more?"

"Maybe a little more while you're up there," said Tom. Nell grabbed the branch above her head, pulled herself over and up to stand like she was using a gymnastic parallel bar. She easily straightened up and cut down more vine.

"You should see how far I can see up here, even in the dark," she commented.

"No thanks!" said Ned, not a lover of heights.

"Can you see Zephram?" Lizzie asked wistfully. Nell turned her head to look.

"No, I think we're too far away already."

"Which is a good thing," Tom reminded them, grunting as he struggled with the logs. "Okay, Lizzie, hold that end while I wrap this end," he instructed. Nell dropped lightly to the ground and joined the three to wind and tie the vine around the logs. In surprisingly little time, they had made a raft that was maybe 6' x 9'.

"Help me pull it over here," Tom directed them toward a spot on the shore that was less rocky.

"I don't think it's big enough to hold all of us," Lizzie said doubtfully.

"That's okay, it doesn't really have to," Tom said. "You and Nell can sit on it. I don't think the water's that deep, see the rocks in the middle? We'll put all our supplies on top with you two, and then Ned and I will walk or swim along and push you by holding the edge."

"If you think so," Lizzie said, hardly any more enthusiastic. The four carefully loaded up the raft at the shore line. Then, Lizzie and Nell waded in and gingerly climbed on. The raft dipped slightly under their weight, but straightened out after they balanced themselves. Most importantly, it didn't sink!

"Here goes," said Ned as he and Tom pushed off and grabbed a hold of the sides. After several tense minutes, they made it safely to the other side. The boys pulled the raft up onto the shore.

"We should hide it so no one sees it," Lizzie said after they removed their belongings.

"Who knows – we might need to use it again on our way back," said Ned. They pulled the raft back into the underbrush and pulled some branches and dead leaves over it.

"*Now* can we sleep?" asked Nell.

"In a moment," said Tom. He and Ned quickly changed into dry clothes in the darkness. Then the quadruplets assembled their things and went back into the trees that blanketed the side of the river. After walking about 100 yards to get safely out of sight, they found soft grasses, perfect for settling down for a few moments of sleep while waiting for the first light of day.

Chapter Twelve

Mid-morning found the quadruplets refreshed and munching on their usual sandwiches, as they consulted Tom's map and compass.

"I think we'll be fine if we keep going that way," Tom said, lining up his compass and pointing toward the East.

"How much longer?" asked Lizzie.

"Maybe two more days," Tom decided, referring to the map again.

"You keep saying that," Ned pointed out.

"Well, it's my best guess. It depends on how fast we're walking," said Tom, irritated. "Walk faster, maybe we'll reach them sooner."

"Okay, okay, I get it," said Ned.

"Then let's get going," said Nell, and she started putting her things away.

After they had gathered up their belongings, the quadruplets started on their way again, walking under cover of the sparse forest as much as they could. It was an uneventful morning, until …

"What's that sound? Do you hear it?" Ned asked, stopping in his tracks.

"I don't hear anything," said Nell.

"Wait," said Lizzie, "I *feel* it, can't you?" Tom and Nell frowned while Lizzie and Ned looked at each other in agreement.

"The sound must be vibrating in the ground," Lizzie continued. "I wonder what it is."

"I think it's coming from over there," Ned pointed. "Let's go."

Tom and Nell shook their heads.

"You can't just run over there," Tom cautioned. "We need to be careful. It could be a trap."

Suddenly, Nell stopped.

"I can hear it, too," she said. "Tick, tock, tick, tock … it sounds like a big clock. Hurry up." Ignoring Tom, she pushed past Ned and Lizzie to lead the way toward the sound.

Suddenly, the trees gave way to a wide open meadow, and right smack in the middle of the meadow was a great – no, huge – old oak tree.

The noise the children had heard and felt was indeed the *tick tock* of a clock. There it was, in the middle of the oak tree's trunk. Hanging next to clock was a wheel with big numbers on it. The wheel seemed to be moving slowly, rotating past a tree limb that looked like it was a marker the numbers would pass as the wheel turned.

"What's this?" Tom asked.

"Hey, my watch is off," Ned said, taking care of practical business and adjusting his watch to match the big clock's time.

"You know," Tom said, looking at the number on the wheel and counting on his fingers, "I think that number's the day. It must be some sort of calendar."

"Let's check it out," urged Nell, walking closer. And the closer they got, they saw how big the tree really was.

In fact, it was as big as a fortress and they could see the outline of a door under the clock face.

Suddenly, the door popped open and out came an old man, dressed like a wizard with a pointy gold hat and a brilliant blue robe encrusted with stars.

He consulted the clock above his head, turned and saw the children, and cried:

"There you are, I've been waiting! Just in time, come in, come in!"

"Who are you?" Nell asked him suspiciously. The quadruplets wisely didn't budge.

"Who am I?" the old man repeated, in a surprised tone of voice. "Who am I?" he repeated yet again.

"Yes, who are you?" Tom asked.

"You don't know who I am?" he tried one more time.

"Nope," said Nell.

"Not a clue," Tom added.

"Why – I'm the History Writer," he declared importantly, with a dramatic flourish as he swept his left hand in front of him.

"What's a history writer?" asked Lizzie.

"Not *a* history writer – *the* History Writer," the History Writer corrected with annoyance. Still the four looked at him blankly. "I write the history," he tried again. Still no luck. "*Your* history." Nothing. "The History of Ancient Zephram," he said with disgust.

"Oh, *that* history," said Tom.

"I *hate* that book," said Ned. "*You're* the one who writes it? Listen, Mr. History Writer, there's way too much – too much history in it!"

"And what's wrong with that?" asked the History Writer sternly. "I should think as you are a Prince of Zephram, you should want to know all about your history."

"We leave that to Tom," said Ned.

"Wait, you know who we are?" Tom realized.

"Of course I know who you are. '*The un-magical royal quadruplets who can't do any tricks ... over one thousand years of magic ... what about the prophecy ... what about the kingdom ... if they're not magical, what are we going to do ... no one must know about the prophecy ... *' I know it all. I just finished up your latest chapter when you came through the trees – here, I'll show you," he gestured for them to follow him into the door in the giant tree.

Still the children hesitated.

"I'm <u>not</u> with Prince Persius," the History Writer assured them. "I don't make history, I just write it down. You are safe with me – although your parents and your sister back in Zephram, I'm not so sure." He shook his head.

That got the quadruplets moving after him through the door and into the tree.

"What about them?"

"What can you tell us?"

"What do you know?"

"Here, you can read what's happened since you left, up until you just met me here outside. It's hot off the press, as you can see."

All around the room they had just entered in the trunk of the vast tree, the children could see pens scribbling. The pens were frantically racing back and forth across pages and pages of paper.

"What is this place?" Ned asked, momentarily diverted. Of course, being inside a tree, it looked like a tree house. There wasn't any furniture in this big, main room. It appeared to house more piles of paper and dancing pens than the children could count, and nothing else. The only people in the room were the quadruplets and the History Writer, and they could feel and hear the steady *tick tock* of whatever the huge calendar clock thing was.

"This is where all the History of the World is written down as it happens."

"The whole world?"

"Yes. There's Zephram's history, over here." The History Writer walked over to one side and carefully retrieved completed pages from the pile in front of Zephram's racing pen. "That's how I knew you had finally arrived," he explained, pointing at a line on a page. Sure enough, the four saw their names right on the paper, the ink barely dry.

"May we read it?" Tom asked.

"Please go ahead. But let's just wash your hands first, shall we?" he said, taking a good look at the quadruplets' grubby appearance, and slightly worried about his pristine pages and how they would survive the most enthusiastic reading by Royal Children *ever* in the history of Zephram!

After soaping up and drying off, the four huddled around the pages, eager, yet afraid, of what they might discover as they read.

There was Prince Persius's takeover, with Tom and Ned's unsuccessful visit to their father chronicled first. Then they read how they had led the soldiers back and forth and back and forth through the Royal Forest; then, the smelly Bog Marsh was mentioned, and even how they had fooled the guards with the Wild Hydrox. Every minute of what they had done was written in sharp, sparse detail.

But then they read also about their parents' continued stay in the dungeon; the increasing of the ransom amount due at the end of the Month of Zephram Mondays; and last, which brought a big laugh from them, of Zephera bravely continuing to refuse to marry Prince Persius and slipping a powder in his drink that caused him to spend most of the day in the Royal Toilet.

"Wow! It's all there," Nell said. "What they're doing –"

"*And* what *we're* doing," Tom realized. "These pages get delivered to our castle every week. Remember how it gets brought to us in the Royal Schoolroom? Mr. History Writer, if you send this, Prince Persius will know that we are still alive, and going for help."

"Can you tell us what *will* happen?" asked Lizzie.

"No, I can only tell you *as* it happens." He looked over at all the busy pens. "I can't change history. But I can be a little late in delivering it," he decided. "Now, you must be hungry."

"Starving," said Ned.

"Then come away from the pages and let's see what we can get you to eat."

After a simple but filling meal of flora-ora fritters and juice, the quadruplets knew they had to get on their way.

"Why don't you come with us?" Lizzie asked the History Writer. "We're just children. We could use all the help we can get."

"Gracious, no, child," he cried, offended. "I am the History Writer. I can't possibly leave, I've got history to write."

"But, you'll wait to deliver the newest history pages to Zephram until you read what we're doing," Tom reminded him.

"Yes, I'll wait," the History Writer agreed. "Never did like Persius. I wanted Zephera to marry that Duke Harry. She met him at her third birthday, you know."

"Yes," said Nell, and Lizzie smiled as they both remembered Zephera saying just that!

"It's the least I can do. I'm a big fan of your father's, too," said the History Writer. "I think he's done great things for Zephram. Is Zephera as pretty as my pen writes?"

"Yes," said Lizzie, loyally. The History Writer was quiet for a moment.

"Not quite sure what you quadruplets can to do to save the day," he said eventually, looking at the four little faces in front of him. "But *I* don't predict the history," he reminded them. "What happens is all up to you. Here, take some of this bread and some more of this flora-ora butter."

"Oh, good, we were running low," Ned said, grabbing the supplies. Lizzie frowned at him because of his rudeness. "Thank you," he added.

Last, the History Writer helped them fill up their water bottles.

"Good luck to you, your Highnesses," he said, glancing at the latest pages. "The coast is clear. None of Persius's forces are around here or looking for you. They are back at the castle. That was good thinking to use the Wild Hydrox."

"Thank you for your help, Mr. History Writer," the quadruplets said in unison, and they resumed their trip. Soon, the *tick tock* of the giant clock in the tree faded out of their hearing. Well-fed and reassured by the pages of the *History of Ancient Zephram* that, for the time being, their parents and Zephera were as safe as could be expected, *and* that no one was after them, they were able to continue their journey with renewed energy.

Understandably, they still kept off of any major paths and roads, depending on the compass and the map to lead them in the right direction. That worked well for quite awhile, until the quadruplets got to a major road which they had no choice but to cross.

"*Now* what should we do?" Nell asked.

Tom carefully looked around them. It was dark now that the sun had set. They'd been walking for a long time.

"At least it's nighttime. Looks like the coast is clear," he said. "Why don't we cross over and then we can stop for a rest once we're out of the view of the road and no one can see us."

"It's about time," Nell grumbled. "Tramp, tramp, tramp – you're such a drill sergeant."

"Of course he is," Ned sprang to his defense, while Tom just ignored her. "He has to be. You want to take your good old time to rescue Mom and Dad?"

"Right, of course I do," Nell said sarcastically. "I'm sure they're not uncomfortable in the dungeon, and Zephera really doesn't mind marrying Prince Persius! Look, I'm just tired and my feet hurt and I have a blister on my heel. And I'm worried, that's all. Aren't you?"

Lizzie interrupted them to change the subject. "I'm not tired," she said, "and I don't even think it's been very scary."

"You *don't?*" asked a voice in the darkness that *wasn't* Tom, Ned or Nell!

Chapter Thirteen

Lizzie let out a shriek and moved in close to Tom, Ned and Nell.

"Who's there?" Tom asked, managing to get control of his voice.

"I am."

"No, I am."

"No, I am." Three separate voices argued with each other, and a massive shape separated from the shadows. In the dim moonlight, the quadruplets could see that the shape was a big three-headed Ogre with one blonde head, one brown head, and one red head.

"Great, and things were going so well up until now," Ned said sarcastically.

"Who are you?" Tom asked.

"I'm Hugo," said the left blonde head.

"No, *I'm* Hugo," said the right brown head. "You're Hershel."

"But I want to be Hugo, not Hershel."

"But it's my turn."

"I'm Hershel," said the middle red head. "You two are idiots. I am *always* Hershel, no matter who you think you are. But, who are *you?*" he continued, taking a step closer to the children. "Children out past their bed time – ah, ah, ah! They might end up being a midnight snack for someone."

"Not us, we don't eat kids," the one who wanted to be Hugo said, completely ruining Hershel's effect.

"But we _do_ want your money," said Hershel, as the Ogre's left hand came up and smacked Hugo in the head.

"Ow," said Hugo, the right head.

"Why?" asked Ned.

"Because you want to cross over our road and that costs money," Humphrey, the left head who wanted to be Hugo, pointed out helpfully.

"It's not _your_ road, it's my Da–" Tom stopped himself just in time. He didn't want any of the heads – Hugo, Hershel or Humphrey – to know who they were.

"Of course it's our road," said Hershel. "We're a big mean Ogre and you're four little kids. If we say you have to pay us money to cross our road, you _have_ to pay us money to cross our road."

"But we don't have any money to give you," said Nell bravely.

"No money?" asked Humphrey, who wanted to be Hugo.

"We're just kids," said Tom.

The three heads considered this.

"They're probably right."

"Yeah, we never had money when we were kids, either."

"I wish we ate kids. That would be easier."

"How about your knapsack?"

"I want my knapsack," said Ned, to whom the question was addressed.

"Then it looks like you're not going across our road," said Hershel.

"I know, I have an idea. How about a magic deck of cards instead of money?" Ned offered.

"Hum, magic … now that would be fun," said Hugo.

"I love cards," said Humphrey who wanted to be Hugo.

"Hand them over," said Hershel, "and then we'll see." Ned handed them over.

"These don't look magic," said the one who was Hershel.

"What you do is deal them and the first one to grab an ace is the winner," Ned instructed them.

"Winner of what?" asked Hershel suspiciously.

"The winner of the magic cards, of course," said Ned. He took the cards back, and then he carefully started dealing the cards onto the ground in front of the Ogre. "King, Two, Jack, Seven, Ace –"

"I got it!" shrieked Hugo, grabbing the card with the Ogre's right hand.

"No, it's mine," said Humphrey.

"Give it to me," said Hershel, as the left hand came up to try to wrestle the card away from the right hand. Before the quadruplets' astonished eyes, the Ogre got into a huge fight with himself, as the right hand and left hand kept grabbing the card from each other. The heads' snarled and leaned in to bite the hands and arms; then suddenly, the Ogre fell to the ground amid yells and grunts from its three heads, and continued fighting himself.

Ned tossed the rest of the cards down next to the Ogre.

"Let's go," Tom urged them, and they bolted across the road while the Ogre was distracted

"Great job," Nell congratulated Ned.

"Thanks."

"I wasn't sure what you were up to there," admitted Tom.

"Neither was I. I was just stalling for time," Ned confessed. "Then I remembered the one time when I pulled that same card game to fool that stupid Alf. Can you believe he fell for it, too?"

"No way," said Nell admiringly. "Do you think Alf's in the dungeon too?"

"Oh, I hope so. And Amaralyn and —"

"You don't mean that!" Lizzie interrupted Ned, horrified.

"Well, *I* mean it," said Nell. "After how nasty they are to us, and never getting in any trouble for it? Serves them right."

"If it's bad for *them* in the dungeon, it'll be just as bad or worse for Mom and Dad and Zephera," Tom reminded Nell and Ned.

"Oh, well, then, I guess I hope *no one's* in the dungeon, or at least no one's in the dungeon being tortured or starved, even if they deserve it," Nell said with a pout.

"Do you think that ogre man thing will come after us?" Lizzie asked, looking worriedly over her shoulder.

"I don't know," Tom admitted. "Let's get as far away from them as we can. If they do, I'm sure they may not be so glad to see us again."

"Don't worry, I'll save us again," said Ned, and charged confidently ahead of them.

Finally the quadruplets found a low wall of shrubs that hid them from sight in the bright moonlight, and they were able to curl up with their heads pillowed on their knapsacks for the rest of an uneventful night.

Chapter Fourteen

The next morning, as was quickly becoming his habit, Tom pulled out the map and his compass to check their progress.

"Looks like we're getting pretty close," Lizzie commented as she leaned over his shoulder to look.

"I bet we'll get there early this afternoon," Tom said. "Yep, just one more thing to get through."

"One more thing to get through?" Ned repeated suspiciously. "What's that?"

"Well, an obstacle. Actually, it may not be an obstacle," said Tom. "If it's not there when we get there, then it wouldn't be an obstacle at all."

"What's *it?*" asked Ned.

"We might run into the Borneo Boar, right about *here,*" Tom said over-casually, pointing on the map at the small pen strokes representing trees in an area called Borneo Bush.

"Since when are we anywhere near the Borneo Boar?" Nell demanded.

"You know, if any of you had paid attention to our geography lessons, you wouldn't be so surprised all the time," Tom commented. "Chances are we won't even see it, so why worry?"

"Oh, yeah, that's the way our luck goes," Ned said sarcastically. "It's not like our country has been invaded and attacked, or our parents are in a dungeon, or we had to escape at night from the people who want to 'dispose' of us, or we've been walking for hundreds of miles to get help –"

"Only like 50 or so miles," Tom interrupted helpfully.

"So, yeah, chances are we *wouldn't* run into the Borneo Boar?"

"Yeah, right," agreed Nell.

"But we might not run into it," Tom pointed out.

"What should we do about it?" Lizzie asked, ever practical. "Just in case we do," she added, smiling at Tom.

All Zephram children knew about the Borneo Boar, the wild pig with the huge tusks that lived all by itself in the Borneo Bush.

It lived all by itself because anytime that people came near the Borneo Bush, the Borneo Boar would sneak up on them and use its huge sharp tusks to help *encourage* them to leave.

It could see in the dark and seemed to have eyes in the back of its head, so no one could hide from it. And, it could smell people who were just *thinking* maybe they'd drive past Borneo Bush on their way somewhere else – and *presto*, it would be waiting for them.

It was big, ugly, smelly, and dangerous, and its tusks, when it 'encouraged' people to leave, *hurt!* Plus, it also wasn't fond of sharing the Bush with any other animals or creatures, so it had plenty of opportunity to keep its tusks well-sharpened from 'encouraging' them to leave.

Now, truthfully, the magical people of Zephram could just throw up an invisible barrier that kept the Borneo Boar a good tusk's length away. It was annoying, but it worked just fine, so they could go through the Borneo Bush if they needed to, instead of traveling much longer around it.

However, non-magical people (such as people from the rest of the world, and, of course, the quadruplets) weren't so lucky.

"Do we have to go through Borneo Bush?" Ned asked. "Couldn't we just go around it?"

"We could but it will take us a lot longer. Really, what are the chances we'll see the Boar? Not everyone sees it."

"You mean 'gets attacked by it,' I think," said Nell.

"Everybody sees it," said Ned.

"We can walk really fast, and run if it sees us. I bet at least one of us will make it out and find Duke Harry," said Tom.

"That's a dumb plan," said Ned.

"I don't think we should wander through the Bush, and just hope we don't see it or it doesn't see us, or we just run," said Nell.

"Then what should we do?" asked Tom. They were quiet for a couple of minutes, stumped.

"Okay – then what about this: How about we try to get to it *first* before it gets to us?" Tom asked.

"Can we do that?" Lizzie asked.

"Let me think for a moment," said Tom, and he propped his elbows on his knees and rested his chin in his hands.

An hour later, after Tom was done thinking and his brother and sisters had finished arguing with him, they stepped carefully and quietly into the Borneo Bush. They looked around and listened for any noise. They didn't see or hear anything, and they decided the coast was as clear of the Borneo Boar as it could be. Very soon, they were lucky enough to enter an area that looked perfect for their plan.

The other night when they had made the raft to cross the river, Tom had saved the extra vine Nell had cut down from the tree. Now he took the vine out of Nell's knapsack, wrapped it around Ned's waist and made a secure knot.

Meanwhile, Nell nimbly climbed up a tall tree at the edge of the clearing. The tree had a big strong limb stretching over the open space below. She settled comfortably on the branch and waited for Tom to toss the other end of the vine up to her. Once she grabbed it, she tossed it over top of the branch above her to create a pulley system.

Lizzie and Tom climbed up Nell's tree to wait for the action, leaving Ned down on the ground. (Ned, always up for an adventure, had volunteered to be their bait to attract the Boar!) Lizzie settled in partway up, while Tom carefully joined Nell on the higher branch.

Ned stood sheepishly clutching the odd tools that would hopefully save him from his Borneo Boar attack:

flora-ora butter sandwiches that were soft, oozing, squishy, and sticky.

"Be careful," Lizzie said, unnecessarily.

"I'm fine," Ned said, brazening it out. "Just pull me up fast, you hear," he said sternly to Tom and Nell, because that was their big part of the rescue plan: hoisting Ned out of danger. "I can't believe I let you talk me into this."

Nell snorted. "Right – you *insisted*, remember?"

"Shush," hissed Lizzie.

There was a long moment of quiet. And then,

"Say something, someone," said Ned, a little nervously.

"Here, Boar, Boar, Boar," Nell called.

"Here, Boar, Boar, Boar," Lizzie continued. Nothing happened.

"Come out, come out wherever you are," Nell said. Nothing happened.

"I'm bored," said Ned. "How much longer … "

Suddenly, the Borneo Boar bolted out of the shadows, snarling and snapping as it charged toward Ned. It was as ugly, big and scary-looking as the quadruplets had heard.

"Pull him up!" shrieked Lizzie.

"Pull me up!" yelled Ned.

"Throw it <u>now</u>!" Tom demanded when, with a mighty pull, he jerked Ned off the ground, out of harm's way. Just as Ned was lifted up, the boar lunged to snap at Ned, and into the wide opened jaws below, Ned dropped his big, squishy sandwich.

The Borneo Boar stopped in its tracks, surprised that its mouth was full of something other than a boy!

It started shaking its head, and then it started banging its head on the ground to try to loosen everything that was stuck together with flora-ora butter. Then, it tried to knock its tusks into the ground to help pry its jaw open because its teeth and jaws were practically glued together with the flora-ora butter sandwich, which was worse than peanut butter for sticking power.

"How much flora-ora butter did you use?" Nell asked Ned.

"A whole jar," said Ned, dangling out of reach of the pre-occupied Boar. "Tom, get ready, I think I'm near enough," he said.

Thunk.

Another whole jar of the precious flora-ora butter was gone as Ned threw it and it effectively smacked the Boar on the head just as Tom hauled him out of the Boar's range again. After a very long moment,

THE BORNEO BOAR COLLAPSED FROM BEING HIT ON THE HEAD!

The four held their breaths for what seemed an eternity. In the sudden silence, they could hear the birds chirping, the wind rustling and the Borneo Boar's labored breathing.

"I think you got it," said Tom, lowering Ned to the ground. "Let's get out of here! I just hope it will be unconscious long enough for us to make it through the Bush."

"Good job!" Lizzie said to Ned, as they quickly climbed down and joined him.

"Thanks," said Ned, unraveling the vine from around his waist. They gave the Borneo Boar one last look and ran off into the trees. "We're out of flora-ora butter," he observed sadly. "I hope Duke Harry has something to eat." They headed for the border of the Borneo Bush, hurrying to get beyond it before the Boar woke up.

Within a half an hour, they broke, huffing and puffing, out of the Bush into safety.

"Looks like we should find Duke Harry soon, if they're on their way back from the tournament like they should be," Tom commented, taking a long drink of his water as he looked at his map.

"Any more obstacles we might run into? Anything you want to tell us about?" Nell asked sarcastically.

"None," said Tom. "That I know of," he added, after a quick pause.

"Ha, ha," said Ned.

"Do you think Duke Harry will be easy to find?" Lizzie asked.

"I'm not sure." Tom considered. "I bet they've been practicing their maneuvers. Wearing camouflage, you know."

Chapter Fifteen

As it turned out, the troops and Duke Harry were quite easy for the quadruplets to find, a mere twenty minutes later.

Why? Because they were sitting right out in the open of a big field, dazzlingly attired in their eye-catching red, white and gold uniforms. And, if that wasn't enough, they had erected their tents, *and* their beautiful maroon flags (the ones with the blue unicorns and gold stars) were fluttering gaily, proudly and obviously in the wind.

"Camouflage?" Nell laughed. Duke Harry heard them at the exact moment they saw them, and he quickly jumped up from amongst the circle of soldiers he was sitting with in the clearing.

"Tom! Children! What are you doing here?" he asked, surprised.

"We're here to get <u>you</u>," Tom said.

"Get me?" Duke Harry repeated.

The quadruplets stumbled over themselves in their hurry to tell their unbelievable story.

"Prince Persius ... "

" ... Mom and Dad ... "

" … Month of Mondays … "

" … 30 billion florites … "

" … Dungeon … "

" … We saw the ships … "

" … No one believed us … "

" … Escape … "

" … Get help … "

" … Zephera … "

"What about Zephera?!?" Duke Harry broke in abruptly.

"Well," Lizzie bit her lip.

"Calm down and tell me everything, one at a time," he sternly directed them. So they did. At the end of their tale, they looked expectantly at Duke Harry.

"So let's get going," Ned said, glad and relieved that he and his brother and sisters had completed *their* part of the mission successfully, and were now able to hand it over into Duke Harry's capable, grown-up hands.

"Well, the problem is, I'm not sure that we can," Duke Harry unexpectedly replied.

"What?" the quadruplets all exclaimed, shocked and incredulous. Given Duke Harry's perfect history – his successful wooing of Princess Zephera, his hero status, his incredibly handsome good looks, his military reputation – his answer was beyond bizarre.

"Your news certainly explains everything that's been happening here," Duke Harry continued, despite the children's outburst. "We've lost *our* magic, too."

"You did?"

"Yes, it's completely gone."

"Well, I'm sure that's a shame for you," said Nell, "but what does that have to do with helping us rescue everyone?"

"Because I don't think we can *do* anything," Duke Harry admitted sheepishly. "Or, it might be sort of *impossible* to do anything."

"What do you mean, 'you can't do anything,' Duke Harry?" asked Ned.

"I mean our magic is gone, so we can't *do* anything."

"Okay, I hear you, but I don't understand how that matters," Tom said.

"Since you're not magical, I guess you don't know how much we use our magic, or how much our magic does for us. Let me try to explain." Duke Harry paused for a moment to think his answer through.

"See the horses?"

"Yes," they said.

"We don't actually know how to ride them."

"You don't?" asked Ned, incredulously.

"No, it's just magic. And, our swords," he patted his own at his side. "I haven't the faintest idea how to use it." Then he pointed over at the black cauldron resting on top of some charred remains of a fire. "We're starving. We haven't eaten in days since the fire went out."

"So you really can't do anything at all," Lizzie said sadly.

Duke Harry nodded, embarrassed.

"What's the good of having a warrior duke in the family if he can't *do* anything?" Ned muttered.

"*Almost* in the family," Nell reminded him in a whisper. "Maybe Zephera won't want him when she hears he's useless!"

"Let me think about this for a moment," Tom said, leaving Duke Harry and his brother and sisters to go sit on a fallen log, a few feet away.

"Well, I don't care if you're magic or not," Lizzie said valiantly, ever optimistic. "I'm just glad we finally found you. I know Tom will figure something out. He always does."

But the first thing Tom said when he was done thinking was, "Let's make some dinner." It was a good suggestion. Everyone would feel better after some food in their stomachs.

"How are we going to do that?" asked Duke Harry. "There's no fire, and the magic cauldron isn't working."

"It doesn't look magic to me," pointed out Nell. "It just looks like any old cauldron. Pots don't need to be magic to cook, you know. It just needs stuff in it to cook once we get a fire started."

"But what 'stuff' will you put in it?" Duke Harry asked, curious.

"What do you have?" asked Lizzie.

"Um, well, nothing," said Duke Harry. "That's the problem. Normally we don't need to carry much food with us. We just wave a hand and say, "Soup pot jack pot meeno mumbo chi," and it's filled with flora-ora stew. And I just snap my fingers for the fire to start."

"That's it? Man, you magical people sure have it easy," Ned commented enviously.

"I suppose you use magic to take care of the horses, too," Tom said.

Duke Harry looked sad and embarrassed at that, because a military man always takes care of his horse. "Yes, I'll admit we've had some trouble controlling them without magic. Although at least *they're* not hungry, they've been eating grass."

"I hate to break it to you," said Nell, "but that's what we'll probably be eating too."

Duke Harry looked horrified.

"Unless you'd rather keep starving," she added. Duke Harry swallowed.

"We've been eating flora-ora butter for days," Lizzie said. "Some hot soup made with grass or vegetables will be a nice change."

"My men and I could just eat the flora-ora butter if you'd rather have the soup," Duke Harry said, his eyes lighting up.

"So sorry, we've used it all," Ned said, not at all sorry in the least.

"The soup won't be so bad," Lizzie promised. "Who will get some water for us?"

"I will. Come on, let's get started." Ned hopped up to help supervise some of the soldiers as they filled their water bottles from the nearby pond and emptied them in the cauldron.

"Does anyone want to know how to start a fire?" Tom asked, crouching down at the base of the cauldron. Duke Harry and several others gathered to watch as Tom set to work. He carefully pulled the lens out of his astrolabe and squinted up at the sky. He positioned the lens so that it caught a strong ray of sunshine, and concentrated the beam on a small pile of dry leaves and twigs.

After a few tense moments, the small pile began to smolder. Then it suddenly burst into flame.

"Magic!" gasped the men, in awe.

"Men, rejoice! Our magic is back!" declared Duke Harry.

"It's not magic," Tom laughed, "it's just science." He carefully nursed the flame, guarding it with cupped hands until it caught hold. "It's just the heat of the sun, magnified by the lens. I learned it years ago. Didn't you?"

"Yes, I'm sure I did," said Duke Harry, "but, you see, magic —"

"Right, magic did it for you. Well, you can do this. Really. Anyone can do it." Duke Harry and the men looked doubtful.

"You'll see. You should try it next time."

"If you think so," said Duke Harry doubtfully. Nell and Lizzie excitedly joined the group around the pot and little fire.

"Look what we found!" Nell exclaimed, thrusting out a fist full of what appeared to be dirty roots and twigs.

"Those are dirty roots and twigs," Duke Harry helpfully pointed out.

"No, these are carrots and potatoes, and green onion grass," Lizzie corrected cheerfully. "We just have to wash them off and cut them up for our soup. It's going to be great! Let's see, how many of us are there?

One, two, three … " she scanned the group and the others down by the pond. "Looks like there's about 24 of us altogether."

"Do you think this is enough?" Nell asked. "We should probably get more. Come on." The two girls dashed off to gather more vegetables. Duke Harry and his men looked disgustedly at the little pile the girls left behind.

"Those weeds are not possibly edible," one soldier commented.

"It sure isn't flora-ora," said the second soldier.

"You're kidding me," said another.

"No way, I'd rather starve," said a fourth.

"You can't expect us to eat that," said a fifth.

"Suit yourselves," said Tom, unconcerned. He and Ned joined their sisters in their search, and soon they had a sizeable pile of vegetables. The water in the cauldron had started simmering. After cleaning the vegetables and borrowing one of the soldiers' useless swords to cut them into smaller pieces, the children dropped the vegetables into the pot.

"This sure would go faster if they helped," Ned grumbled as they looked at the soldiers, who were despondently lounging around, doing nothing.

"Give them a little time," Tom counseled. "I'm sure they'll come around once they smell it cooking. I'm just afraid that they may not be quite as much help as we thought."

"No kidding," said Ned. "What gave it away? The fact that they can't fight?"

"Or ride a horse," added Nell.

"Or cook," added Lizzie.

"Or start a fire," added Nell

"Or do *anything* at all," Ned grumbled. "Everyone gives *us* such a hard time because we can't do magic – playing tricks on us ... "

"Laughing at us," added Lizzie.

"Thinking they're so special," added Nell.

"Being magic hasn't done them any good right now, has it? Looks like *we're* the special ones now!" crowed Ned.

"Then why are *we* doing all the work?" Nell demanded.

"Like I said, give them a little time. I'm sure they'll come around," Tom said.

Soon, the soup was bubbling away inside the big cauldron, and its aroma filled the air. Not surprisingly, the soldiers weren't quite so inclined to turn their noses up at the rustic stew. In fact, after just a few moments, they were lingering quite close to the cauldron, warming their hands and eyeing the soup with anticipation.

"Gosh, how will we eat our soup?" Lizzie asked suddenly. "I don't suppose you've got any bowls and spoons?" she asked Duke Harry. "We couldn't bring them when we escaped. Just that one knife for the flora-ora butter sandwiches."

"Or do they magically disappear when you don't need them?" Nell asked sarcastically.

"Actually, we do have bowls and spoons," Duke Harry said, "but, uh, they're dirty since we couldn't – uh, wish them clean or wish them away."

"Figures," said Ned.

"Well, let's get them and wash them in the pond," said Lizzie in no-nonsense tones.

The soldiers didn't exactly leap up to help. They all kind of looked at each other in dismay. It was obvious what was going through their heads: soldiers don't wash dishes and spoons ... soldiers aren't told what to do by a little girl, even if she was one of their princesses ... soldiers aren't –

"The sooner the bowls and spoons are clean, the sooner you can eat," Tom said, cutting into their thoughts. Up popped the soldiers to get the bowls and spoons, which was a relief to Tom, because he hadn't wanted to pull rank on them as their Crown Prince and heir to the throne ... *unless* he had to.

Soon enough, Duke Harry, the soldiers and the quadruplets were enjoying hearty helpings of the girls' delicious vegetable soup, in clean bowls, with clean spoons. And then second helpings. And then some soldiers (including a couple of the doubters) even had thirds! Not bad for a soup with only three ingredients, none of which was flora-ora.

Chapter Sixteen

By the time dinner was over, the sun had set and the lightning bugs were dancing around the clearing. The quadruplets and Duke Harry settled close to the low burning fire. Everyone was in a better mood now that they'd had followed Tom's suggestion to have something to eat.

"I've been wondering how you found us today," Duke Harry said. "You told me *why* you came to find us, but I'm sort of stumped over *how* you managed to find us." The four looked at him blankly.

"What do you mean by 'how,' exactly?" asked Tom, baffled.

"How did you find us?" repeated Duke Harry. "My men and I were on our way back from the tournament, which we won, of course –"

"Oh, we knew you would. Congratulations!" declared Lizzie warmly.

"But even though we lost our magic, I'm still surprised you were able to find us. There are so many roads we could have taken. We could have been anywhere. Plus, we're military men trained in the art of warfare and camouflage, and you're children." Missing, but implied, was the word 'just.'

"Well," Tom felt badly for what he was going to say. Duke Harry was a famous warrior, he was going to marry their sister, and he was much older than they, so he hated to tell him the truth.

Stalling for time, Tom leaped up and pulled his map and a pencil out of his knapsack.

"Before we escaped from the castle, I figured out your tournament location over here on the map," he pointed with the pencil, "and then I did some calculations. We knew you had plenty of travel time to waste because you weren't due back until a week before the wedding. I figured you'd want to avoid the Sunoma Desert over here," Tom circled that section with his pencil, "and then we remembered that Zephera wanted a diamond necklace, so I thought you'd stop at the diamond mines over *here*. I figured the horses would travel 50 miles a day, so by my calculations, we'd run into you right about *here*." He pointed to a place on the map that was, unbelievably, right where they were.

"What magic did you use, Tom?" asked Duke Harry in disbelief, for packed away in his bag was indeed a beautiful diamond necklace for his bride-to-be. "You must have used magic, how else could you figure out our path?"

"Well, no magic, just some calculations with algebra and calculus and —"

"Didn't you use astronomy?" reminded Ned.

"Oh, yes I did, you're right, I forgot."

"Amazing," said Duke Harry. "I'm so glad you thought to come to get us to save Zephram from Prince Persius." Duke Harry suddenly seemed less doubtful about his abilities now that his stomach was full. "We must go there quickly. If he harms a hair on Zephera's head —"

"Of course we're going back right away," agreed Lizzie. "Although, the magic thing throws us into a bit of a jam, but I bet we can work something out."

"I will do anything," declared Duke Harry, "and my men will as well. There's only a few of us, not a whole troop, but I'm sure we can defeat Prince Persius. Even without magic."

"Well, maybe, sure, we'll talk about that later," said Tom. "First things first, though, your uniforms — they've got to go."

"What?" harrumphed Duke Harry. "This is my dress uniform. It's what we wear."

"You stick out like a sore thumb," said Ned. "No wonder we found you so easily."

"What's with all the gold braid?" asked Nell. "You look too fancy to do anything."

"All we have to do is blink to make it disappear from sight when it's time for battle," said Duke Harry, defending his uniform. "And Zephera thinks I look very handsome."

"Well, being handsome isn't going to do you much good. Especially when Prince Persius sees you coming from miles away," Lizzie pointed out in her practical way. "I think that Nell and I had better cut off the gold braid tomorrow."

"And maybe dirty you up," added Ned, relishing the thought.

"We are all wasting valuable time talking about something as unnecessary as ruining our uniforms when I should be leaving to save Zephera now!" Duke Harry's voice started to get louder with annoyance at the situation, and worry for Zephera.

"We've been traveling for days to get *here* and we don't want to wait any longer either. But I think we have to change our rescue plans now that your magic's gone," said Tom.

"I don't see how that matters," said Duke Harry stubbornly.

"I think it might matter," said Tom. "You said so yourself when we first found you — that you aren't able to do anything. I hate to say it but it's not like you made it anywhere on your own *without* your magic."

"But we didn't know it mattered," pointed out Duke Harry. "We didn't know why our magic was gone. I thought it might be like a cold or flu. But we knew we had plenty of time to get back before the wedding, so I wasn't worried."

"So what would *you* do, Duke Harry?" asked Ned, curious.

"I'd leave now, of course. I'd ride through the night. We'd attack at the gates and defeat Persius's men. In my red and gold uniform," he added pointedly.

"That sounds great," Lizzie said.

"But it won't work," Tom said. "They'll see you coming and they'll capture you."

"Or *worse*," added Ned with glee.

"I think tomorrow we should do some training," Tom suggested. "Maybe some exercises with your horses, maybe some swordplay – just see how you do."

"But we need to get there <u>now</u>," said Duke Harry.

"I know, but we need to do it *right*," Tom pointed out. "We have to be smart, or it won't work. And we won't get another chance to save everyone, and there won't be anyone left to save us!"

"I'm tired," Lizzie said, rubbing her eyes.

"Let's get some sleep and start fresh tomorrow," Tom suggested.

"All right," agreed Duke Harry. "Just for tonight we'll rest. And then we'll see."

Ironically, although the children were saddened and discouraged by the soldiers lack of magic and the unfortunate turn their rescue mission had taken, just being with the strong, grown-up soldiers made them feel safer. Besides, Tom would think of something. He always did! It was their first good night's sleep in a long while.

Chapter Seventeen

The next morning, Duke Harry woke up soon after sunrise to the hustle and bustle of camp sounds.

"What's for breakfast?" he asked the girls, who had been scavenging again.

"Apples," Lizzie said excitedly. Believe it or not, Duke Harry and the soldiers weren't very excited at the limited breakfast menu.

"Do you think *they* think *we're* whipping up flora-ora cakes? Serves them right if they have soup for every meal!" Nell grumbled. "Hey, shouldn't they be waiting on us? We *are* their princesses, if I remember correctly!"

Ned snorted. "Yeah, like anyone would wait on you!"

"Finish your apple," Tom sternly broke into their discussion. "We've got a lot to do today."

He wasn't kidding.

A few hours later ...

"Man, Tom wasn't kidding when he said there was a lot to do," Ned said as he rejoined the girls.

First thing after breakfast, Duke Harry and his soldiers, with glum looks on their faces, had sadly lined up so that Lizzie and Nell could carefully hack off yards and yards of gold braid with their flora-ora knife.

The soldiers were quite a sorry sight with their uniforms stripped of all sparkle and pizzazz. As each one was finished, he was then sent over to where Ned and Tom were evaluating their skill (or lack of skill) with the horses.

"What should we do with the braid?" Nell had wondered. "Do you think we should throw it out?"

"I think we should keep it," Lizzie had said. "Maybe we'll need it. There's quite a lot of it, and it seems quite strong. Help me wrap it up."

"Sure. And then let's dirty the men up," Nell had said, obviously looking forward to it. "Maybe we could just throw some mud on them to start."

"I don't think you'll need to do that," said Ned, as he re-joined his sisters after having spent time with Tom and the soldiers. He was laughing so hard he could barely stand. "You know when they said that magic helped them ride their horses? Well, that meant that they really can't ride them *at all*. I think they need magic just to stay *on* the horse. They keep falling off into the dirt."

"When they're riding?" asked Nell.

"No, they don't even get that far. Tom gives them a leg up into the saddle and they just keep going over the top and then they fall off the other side. They're going to be so sore! You gotta see it. It's so funny to watch *magical* people who can't do anything!"

The three hurried over to where Tom was patiently trying to help the soldiers – well, not even actually ride yet, as Ned had just reported – but just stay in the saddle. Sure enough, the spectacular uniforms were turning brown from repeated landings in the dirt so there was no need for Nell and Lizzie to help with the 'dirtying' process.

"Ned, come over here so I can show them how to mount the horses again," Tom called. Ned obediently joined him and placed his foot in Tom's clasped hands. Ned then used the leverage to swing himself and his leg up over to settle securely in the saddle. He gave the reins a gentle shake and trotted off.

"Magic!" exclaimed the soldiers in amazement.

"Showoff," laughed Nell.

"It must be magic," said Duke Harry in awe, as he and his men watched Ned urge the horse into a gallop. "But you children aren't magical. How can you do this?"

"It's *not* magic," Tom said patiently. "I told you before, it's just practice. Anyone can learn to do it. I'm hoping even all of *you* can learn to do this sometime really soon. Okay, Duke Harry, let's try it again."

The soldiers gamely practiced until lunch time, trying not to be too embarrassed that even the princesses, little girls, could ride as well as the boys.

It wasn't until after a lunch of apples (after a snack of apples) that Tom mustered up the courage to ask, "So, how are you with those swords?"

The soldiers had removed their swords right after breakfast, when it became clear that they might end up stabbing themselves as they fell off the horses.

The pile of swords glistened temptingly in the afternoon sun. The soldiers eagerly approached the pile and hoisted their arms. But the quadruplets soon realized that the soldiers' swordsmanship skills had disappeared into thin air just as their horseback riding skills had.

"Ow, watch out," Nell winced.

"I can't watch," Lizzie said, covering her eyes.

"I can," Ned said, enjoying the spectacle. To him, it just kept getting better and better with everything the soldiers attempted. In fact, if only his arch enemy, Alf, was here, failing miserably like the soldiers, Ned's enjoyment would be complete!

"No, you can help," Tom said to his unrepentant brother, carefully keeping his distance from the soldiers' awkward thrusts and parries. Of course, after the 'success' of their horseback riding, it was easy to predict just how well the swordplay would go. By mid-afternoon it was time for a break.

"I don't suppose you know any hand-to-hand combat?" Tom asked, without much hope.

The soldiers all looked blankly at him. Tom mentally checked another skill off the soldiers' meager skills list.

"You know, wrestling," he tried explaining further.

"Like this – aaaaaahhhh!" screeched Ned as he launched himself on his brother. Lizzie and Nell rolled their eyes.

"You are so immature," said Nell. After scuffling for a moment, Tom easily pinned Ned to the ground.

"Tom always wins," Lizzie explained to Duke Harry and the soldiers. "I don't know why Ned even tries anymore."

"Ah – but one day, he won't be ready for me," Ned huffed and puffed from the ground.

"I don't think any of us have wrestled in a very long time," said Duke Harry.

"Not since I was a little boy," said one of the soldiers.

"With our magic, we never need to get that close to people," said another.

"We've got our uniforms, too," said Duke Harry.

"Yeah, the beautiful uniforms, we know," said Ned, brushing himself off and getting up.

"Looks like we should practice a little wrestling, too," Tom said. "Now that you're going to get pretty close to Persius's troops, you won't have your magic to keep you safe. I'll bet they would never expect you to be able to fight. That'll surprise them."

At least the soldiers had a little more fun with the wrestling. They took out their horseback riding, bowl scrubbing, swordplay and apple eating frustrations on each other. All in all, they survived the long day without too many cuts (although they did get some bumps and bruises from falling off their horses and the wrestling).

"I've been thinking," Tom said, as they all finally settled down for a hearty dinner of vegetable soup. "I don't think we can head right back to Zephram. You and your soldiers, well –"

"You're not very good," Ned interrupted bluntly.

"Maybe we should do a little more work on the horseback riding and swords before we go," Tom said diplomatically.

"As much as I hate to agree with you," Duke Harry said sadly, "I think you're right. We'll never be able to save Zephram and Zephera like this." There was silence for a couple of moments, and then Lizzie sniffed.

"If you think so," she said, brushing away a few tears of worry for their parents and Zephera. Nell gave her a quick hug.

"I'm sorry we aren't much help to you," Duke Harry said, looking at Lizzie's sad face. "I didn't realize just how badly off we are without our magic."

"You'll be plenty of help. At the very least, now there are 24 of us instead of just four kids. I bet you'll be great in a couple of days."

"Yeah, right," Ned snorted under his breath.

"And *we're* all going to help you get ready," Tom added pointedly. "Plus, it'll be good to rest our feet a little more after our walk here."

"It's been a long day," said Duke Harry, yawning. "I don't suppose you have any more flora-ora cream?" Lizzie and Nell had rationed out their limited supply of bandages and cream to the wounded soldiers right after dinner.

"Here," Lizzie yawned and handed him what was left.

"Hey, leave some for my blisters," Ned said, yawning, too. Then, Nell yawned. And then Duke Harry. And then Tom ... and soon everyone in the camp was yawning.

"We'll practice everything again tomorrow and see how you do. Then we can figure out when we'll be ready to go back home," Tom decided. Finally, everyone agreed it made sense to re-evaluate the situation after practice tomorrow, and they settled down so they'd be well rested for another full day.

Chapter Eighteen

As it turned out, 'tomorrow' turned into 10 more tomorrows before Tom and Duke Harry could both agree that the men were ready to help.

Not only did it take quite awhile to train the men, but they were also slowed down by several days of rain, right smack in the middle of days four, six, seven and nine. Being tired, worried and soaking wet made everyone edgy and restless to get going. (Plus, there was only so much room under the tournament tent!)

By the time Day 10 came, everyone agreed they couldn't spend any more time practicing. If they waited any longer, there was a chance they wouldn't make it back to Zephram in time for the Ransom Payment Day for the Month of Zephram Mondays' proceeds. They had to hope that the soldiers had learned enough to make a difference in the attack.

"We *do* have surprise on our side," Tom said reassuringly before dinner, as he and Duke Harry started to discuss the rescue plan and what exactly they could count on the soldiers being able to do.

"It's been three weeks since we left," Lizzie said. "How much longer will Mom and Dad and Zephera be okay? I bet they're worried about us."

"Nah, they think we were eaten by the Wild Hydrox," Ned said helpfully.

"You're horrid," Lizzie shuddered.

"Zephera knows the Wild Hydrox would never eat us," Nell reassured her. "I'm sure she thinks we've gone to get help."

"I hope so," Lizzie said unhappily.

"What's that smell?" Duke Harry asked suddenly, sniffing appreciatively. Lizzie brightened up.

"Nell and I have a surprise for our last dinner."

"It doesn't smell like apples," said Duke Harry.

"Or soup," Ned pointed out.

"That's because it's fish," Lizzie told them excitedly.

"We saw all these worms after the rain, and we got the idea to use some of your gold braid to make a fishing line with a stick." Nell said. "The fish loved the glitter. They were practically throwing themselves at us."

"Glad it came in handy for something," Duke Harry said ruefully, as he looked down at his dirty, unembellished uniform.

"Tom cleaned the fish for us, and we've been roasting it over the fire," Lizzie finished.

Everyone's spirits perked up when they ate their mouth-watering fish dinner, after days and days of vegetable soup and apples. Even those who hadn't liked fish before gobbled it down!

After dinner, the quadruplets and Duke Harry gathered around Tom's map.

"We took *this* route when we came to find you," said Tom, tracing their journey from Zephram with his finger. "We'd be fine crossing the river but the one big problem I see going back that way is that it would be hard for the horses to cross the Rock Field. Of course, we only led the guards that way so that we could make it look like the Wild Hydrox got us."

"Don't forget the smelly Bog Marsh," Nell said. "I'd love to miss that this time if we can."

"I think if we circled east a bit more this way before looping back, we'd miss the Rock Field, and the Bog Marsh," Tom said. "But we'll still end up in the Royal Woods outside of Malowen's stable, and be able to use our secret entrance."

"The poop door," snickered Ned.

"That way looks longer," commented Duke Harry.

"It is, a little," Tom acknowledged. "But we have your horses to use now."

"Yay!" said Nell.

"We should be able to travel back much faster than we did walking all the way here," said Tom.

"We shouldn't waste any more time," said Duke Harry. "Maybe we *should* try the Rock Field. We could just go slowly across it — or leave the horses behind once we got there."

"I think it will raise Persius's suspicions if he hears that there are some horses running loose."

"Dad would kill us if any of the horses got hurt," added Ned.

"We have five days until the ransom is due, so I think we should play it safe by going this longer way," said Tom.

"All right," Duke Harry reluctantly agreed, "we'll do it your way. My men will be ready to leave at sunrise. I know they'll be glad to finally help save Zephram."

"We have been doing something," said Ned, a little stung. "We've taught you to ride."

"And light a fire," said Nell.

"And use your swords," said Lizzie

"And wrestle," said Ned.

"Okay, okay, you're right – *you* have been doing something," Duke Harry admitted. "Now it's our turn to help. But I do have one question for you, Tom. How are you going to get us there?"

"I'm not sure what you mean," Tom said, frowning. "We'll take this path on the map toward the east first and then we'll –"

"But how will you know that you're following the map?" asked Duke Harry.

"By reading it," said Tom. Duke Harry looked blank.

"Well, I'll also use my compass," Tom expanded, "and then, of course, I like to calculate the logarithm of the arc from the stars on the horizon just to make sure and then –"

"Man, you are such a brainiac!" Ned interrupted, laughing.

"I suppose I should have realized compasses and maps are other things that can work without magic," Duke Harry said.

"Oh!" Tom said, as enlightenment dawned. "You can't use yours without magic?"

Duke Harry shook his head. "Maybe you could show me how to do it?" he asked uncomfortably.

"Of course," Tom said enthusiastically, loving to share his knowledge. He thought how hard all of this was on Duke Harry, unable to do *anything* and having to rely on a bunch of kids to do just about *everything*. "It's so cool when you factor in the degree of the constellation —"

"Maybe we could skip that part," Duke Harry laughed. "Just the basics should do."

"Don't forget, we'll also need to bring along some food. Get more apples and veggies," Lizzie pointed out. "And everyone should fill their water bottles."

"Men, help Princess Lizeta with the food and water," said Duke Harry.

"There are no more apples," called one of the soldiers.

"Sure there are, there's a whole tree full," called Ned.

"No, the branches are empty."

"Just the low branches are empty," said Ned, investigating.

"There's no way to get them down," said the soldier.

"Oh, please. I'll get them," Nell said, popping up.

"Those branches are pretty high, Nell," said Duke Harry. "You can't reach them without magic."

"Those branches?" asked Nell, pointing. "I can. Here I'll show you."

"Tom, I think you should stop her," Duke Harry said as Nell quickly ran over to one of the trees and showed every intention of climbing it. In fact, in a split second she had climbed well above their heads.

"She'll be fine," Tom said, without concern, turning to look back down at the map. "Now, here's how I figured out —"

"But," protested Duke Harry.

"Watch out," Nell cried as she started pulling apples off the branches and tossing them to down to earth.

"Nell!" commanded Duke Harry sternly. "It's not safe, get down now." His soldiers knew that tone of voice well, and they all stopped to look and see what would happen next.

Apparently, nothing. Nell just continued picking and tossing apples.

"She really is okay," Lizzie said.

"She loves this stuff," Ned said. "Wait until she does her flip when she jumps off … "

"Actually, she'll probably do a double," Lizzie said, considering the height of the branches. "She has enough room."

"Nell," tried Duke Harry again in his best commander voice.

"Yes?" she said, pausing for a moment. "Why am I doing all the work? You all better gather these up," she pointed to the ground which was peppered with apples.

Then, she reached up to the tree limb above her, swung around and released herself for a graceful mid-air somersault before she landed on the ground.

"Magic!" said the men in amazement.

"No, not magic, just lots of practice," said Nell. She leaned over to start picking up the fruit. "Come on, help!"

"Men, we'll be leaving at sunrise so be packed and ready to leave camp," said Duke Harry. "And don't miss any of the fruit. So, Tom about that compass … "

Chapter Nineteen

The next morning, Lizzie was the first one up, way before dawn.

"Come on, come on, everyone get up! The sooner we leave, the sooner we'll get back to Mom and Dad and Zephera!"

By the time the first tiny glimpse of the sun appeared, the quadruplets and Duke Harry and his men were all saddled up and ready to go. The children were able to ride as well because Duke Harry had several extra pack horses that had carried their supplies (including the big gold tent from the tournament).

"Sure beats walking," Ned said appreciatively, as their little troop started off on the return leg of their all-important rescue mission.

Now that they were on horseback instead of walking, it was amazing how much ground they covered. Surprisingly, Duke Harry and his soldiers were even able to stay on their horses, too. In fact, when they stopped to take a break and water the horses at a gentle stream, the group had traveled about 20 miles without any falls!

Using horses had another advantage: the Borneo Boar made a menacing growl when it came upon them in the Bush, but it took one look at the sheer volume of men and horses, and left them alone. Ned was pleased by that. Not only were they flat out of their most lethal weapons, the flora-ora butter and its jar, but he had no desire to be bait dangling above a boar, ever again!

Needless to say, everyone was quite optimistic at lunch, at dinner, and even at breakfast the next day. No one even minded the third straight meal of apples (not counting their apple snacks, of course).

So it came as a complete surprise to them on the afternoon of the second easy day when suddenly, the sky darkened over their heads, a huge hot wind stirred up and a loud roar was heard.

"What's that?"

"What's going on?"

"What's happening?" cried everyone.

Almost immediately, their situation became horribly clear. A gigantic, fire-breathing dragon was circling over them, its huge wings stirring up dirt and leaves and other debris, its huge size filling the sky above them, its huge fire breath scorching the ground in front of them.

The group came to an abrupt stop. The horses whinnied and bucked with fear. The soldiers fell back, and some fell off. There was no way they could outrun the dragon and survive.

"Great, this is just great," said Ned, of their newest predicament. "I thought you said the coast was all clear if we went this way and avoided the Rock Field."

"No, I just said this way was clear of rock fields," Tom, honest to a fault, corrected him.

"Ah, what do we have here?" asked the dragon pleasantly, little bursts of flame coming out of his mouth. "A little early for dinner, maybe late for lunch but so many soldiers, children and horses are too big an opportunity to pass up. Maybe it's linner. Or dunch," the dragon considered. "No matter. Now, do you want to be slow roasted or quick fried?"

If possible, the soldiers and Duke Harry fell back even more with fear. As usual, they could be counted on for no help whatsoever.

"Quick fried, I think," the dragon decided for them, when no one spoke up with a preference.

The dragon opened his mouth and took a deep breath. The breath was deep enough to reach the very bottom of his fire-making lungs. When he exhaled, the flames shot out.

Suddenly, they sizzled.

"Honestly," said Lizzie, as she aimed a stream of water from her water bottle into the dragon's wide open mouth, "he's just a lot of hot air!" The water effectively squelched the fire. The dragon gulped and sheepishly backed away.

"Please, be my guests," he said, with little puffs of smoke coming out of his mouth as he stepped aside to allow the group safe passage.

"Thank you," said Lizzie graciously.

"It's magic!" said the soldiers in awe.

"No, it's just common sense," Lizzie said, shaking her head.

"Any *other* surprises?" Ned waspishly asked his brother as headed away from the steamy dragon.

"You know, the map doesn't say *watch out the for the big fire-breathing dragon here*," Tom said to his brother with annoyance.

"Maybe it should," said Nell. "I think a lot of people would find it helpful to know that they could be a shish kabob if they come this way."

"Complain, complain, complain," said Tom, and he urged his horse to a trot so he could get as far ahead of his ungrateful brother and sister as possible.

Fortunately, they had no further mishaps before stopping at nightfall. And more good news: they happened upon a wild tangle of grape vines, which made a welcome change from the apples – and helped to stretch their meager supplies.

The night was a little chillier than usual. Tom and Duke Harry talked about lighting a fire, but they didn't want to attract any other unwanted attention – of the fire-breathing dragon kind or any other kind. But they did set-up the festive tournament tent, which helped keep everyone slightly warmer.

"What's the first thing you want to do when we get back?" Nell asked her brothers and sister as they drifted off to sleep.

"You mean after we've rescued everyone and captured Persius?" asked Tom for clarification.

"Yeah, once we taken care of all that," Nell said.

"I'm going to get a bath," said Lizzie. "We're so dirty I bet Mom and Dad won't even recognize us. I don't think our hair will ever be blonde again."

"I'm going to eat as much flora-ora cakes and candy as I can," said Ned.

"What a surprise!" Nell laughed. "Mr. Sweet-tooth himself!"

"I can't wait to read all about our adventure in the latest *History of Ancient Zephram*," said Tom.

"Speaking of surprises," Ned teased.

"Well, I think the first thing I will do is enjoy my bed!" Nell declared, stretching out on the hard ground with a grimace and a groan, and very shortly later, a <u>snore</u>!

Chapter Twenty

The next day didn't feel much warmer, even when the sun rose high in the sky.

Tom, consulting the map and his compass, set them on a straight course. Soon it became clear that they were heading toward what appeared to be a tiny, blindingly glistening object that was still far, far away on the horizon.

"I don't suppose you know what we're heading toward?" Ned asked, fearing another surprise.

"Nope. The map doesn't say anything," said Tom truthfully.

"How can it be getting colder and colder – with the sun out?" asked Nell, shivering. No one had an answer for her. Within the hour, everyone had to pull out extra clothes from their bags, layering whatever they could find, until they were quite a lumpy, dumpy sight riding across the countryside.

By nightfall, the glistening shape was still very far off, and everyone wondered if they'd *ever* get there! It wasn't until lunchtime the next day that it became overwhelmingly and *shiveringly* clear why it was so cold.

The glistening object was an ice field that stretched as far as the eye could see, with shimmering ice pillars like tentacles reaching far up to the sky.

"So you're telling me the map doesn't say anything about this?" Ned asked Tom suspiciously. "*This* seems pretty big not to be mentioned."

"Not a thing. Here, look if you don't believe me," Tom said, thrusting the map at Ned.

"Hey, there's a big white swoosh mark right here."

"But what does the big white swoosh mark *mean?*" Tom pointed out. "Does it *say* anything?"

"Oh, you're so funny!"

"Boys," cut in Duke Harry. They quieted. "How are we going to get through this? It looks too big to travel around. I bet it could take days, even a week, and we don't have the time."

"I have an idea," said Lizzie. "Let's see, ahem," she cleared her throat. "It's been a few weeks so I may be a little rusty. But it's worth a try. Do, re, mi, fa, sol, la, ti, do," she sang, a quick little scale.

"And *this* is going to help?" Duke Harry asked somewhat sarcastically.

"Lizzie, that's a great idea," said Nell loyally. Lizzie took a deep breath.

"AAAAAAAAAAAAAAAAAAAAAAAAAAAAAA AAAAAAAAAAAAAAAAAAAAAAAAAAAAAAA OOOOOOOOOOOOOOOOOOOOOOOOOOOO OOOOOOOOOOOOOOOOOOOOOOOOOOOO OOOOOOOOOOOOOOOOOOOOOOOOOOOO EEEEEEEEEEEEEEEEEEEEEEEEEEEEEE!"

Lizzie's high, clear voice rang out. After a moment, it was drowned out by the sound of the cracking and the tinkling of ice shattering and falling to the ground.

"Good job!" Tom congratulated her. "You may need to do it a few more times to get us all the way through."

"Sure thing," Lizzie said, clearing her throat again.

"Magic," whispered the soldiers, in awe as they surveyed the wreckage of the ice pillars and the jagged holes Lizzie's voice had opened up.

"Not magic," said Lizzie, "just a lot of practice." She took a deep breath and started singing her high, ice-breaking notes again.

It took until darkness, but the horses were finally able to pick their way carefully over the ice shards to reach the other side.

"I think it's warmer already," Nell declared, but they rode another hour or so before it finally felt comfortable enough to take off any of those lumpy, dumpy layers.

"How much longer *now* 'til we get back to Zephram?" asked Ned as they sat around the luxury of a campfire he had started by carefully rubbing two sticks together, with the friction creating a spark that 'took' on a pile of dead leaves.

"Apple?" Nell offered, opening a sack to hand them around.

"I think we're close enough to get there by tomorrow night," Tom said.

"Oh, then let's not wait," Lizzie cried. "If we're so close, let's get there as soon as we can."

"I know you're excited, but I think we shouldn't go anywhere near Zephram until it's dark."

"Why not?" Lizzie asked.

"Because I don't want Persius to see us and catch us after all this."

"Okay, fine," said Lizzie, disgruntled – she who was never usually disgruntled. She took a bite of her apple and chewed. And bit and chewed some more. Presently, she asked, "What are we going to do once we get there, anyway?"

"Well, you know, lots of stuff, lots of things," said Tom.

"Like what?" asked Nell.

"Uh –"

"When?" asked Lizzie.

"Uh –"

"Where?" asked Ned.

"Uh –"

"How?" asked Duke Harry.

"Okay, so I'm not sure what we're going to do," Tom admitted. "I just know that we have to surprise Prince Persius and his men."

"No, *you think?*" interrupted Ned, sarcastically.

"And get our hands on the Golden Ball," Tom continued.

"Well, *obviously!*" chimed in Nell.

"The only reason Persius was able to pull off the whole invasion is that he had the Golden Ball and the magic stopped when he touched it. He knew everyone in the castle would be helpless without their magic –"

"Helpless?" sputtered Ned, "more like useless!"

"My men and I won't be useless during the rescue," Duke Harry promised a little stiffly.

"Of course you will," Lizzie said warmly in encouragement.

Duke Harry looked shocked, and suddenly Lizzie realized she'd said the wrong thing.

"No, I meant, of course you *won't* be useless," she corrected herself, while Ned and Nell shared an amused glance at Lizzie's slip. "You know there's no way we could do this without you, right?" she said, turning to her brothers and sister for support.

"Yeah, I guess," said Ned ungraciously.

"That's why we came to get you," Tom reminded Duke Harry and the soldiers.

"You've learned a lot, I suppose," said Nell, also ungraciously.

"Thank you," said Duke Harry stiffly. "It's all to save my poor Zephera."

"Together we'll all save *everyone!*" Tom declared.

"Even Alf!" laughed Lizzie.

"I don't think so," said Ned.

"And *not* those horrid girls, either," said Nell.

"We'll save *everyone*," Tom repeated. "Well, I'm going to sleep," he said, clearly wanting to end the various discussions, about both his planning and Duke Harry's readiness. "You know, it may be the last chance we have to sleep until after we've rescued Zephram."

"Wow, you're right!" Ned declared. "We'll finally be there!"

So the quadruplets and Duke Harry and his men settled in for the night, each thinking about the important adventure ahead of them and their role in it. The night passed uneventfully until –

"Humphrey, look who it is!"

Chapter Twenty-One

"I'm Humphrey," said another irritated voice. "Who is it?"

"It's that boy who escaped from us with that card trick."

Ned opened his eyes. Sure enough, looming over him and blocking out the early morning sun, was the three-headed Ogre, Hugo Humphrey Hershel. Ned groaned. Around him he could see Nell and Lizzie and the soldiers groggily looking on in horror.

"Hi, fellas," he said weakly. "What are you doing here? How come you're not guarding your road?" He didn't see Tom anywhere. Just *great*.

"We're on vacation," said the head on the right, whoever he was this time. "Thought we'd check out the ice fields."

"But they were such a disappointment," said the head on the left, whoever he was this time. "It just looked like broken pieces of ice."

"Really," said Ned. "That's a shame."

"Stop talking," said the head in the middle. "We're not falling for any more of your tricks. I think we'll have to reconsider eating children. Of course," he laughed meanly, looking around, "we _do_ eat adults."

"Right," said right.

"We do," agreed left. As could be expected, the soldiers drew back in fear, just the same way they did when they saw the fire-breathing dragon.

"We're very dirty, I don't think we'll taste very good," said Nell helpfully.

"Taste? Who cares how you taste," said middle. "We just like the crunch."

"Do _all_ of you like the crunch?" Ned asked, desperately trying to think of something to stall for time. "Because my bones are still growing. They're kind of soft. I break them all the time."

"He does," agreed Lizzie.

"But if you like the crunch, I bet those guys," he pointed at the soldiers, "I bet _their_ bones are dry and crunchy. So if you all like the crunch, I'd start with them."

"I love the crunch," and "I hate the crunch," said left and right simultaneously while some of the soldiers shuddered and moaned with fright.

"Humphrey, you don't like the crunch?" Ned took a chance and asked of the right head.

"No, _I'm_ Humphrey," said the left head.

"No, it's _my_ turn to be Humphrey," said right.

"You are Hugo," the middle head said decisively to left. "You are Humphrey," he said to right. "And you," he pointed at Ned, "stop confusing them. I know what you're up to."

Ned gulped. Where was Tom?

"Ow," said Hugo. He reached up his right arm and slugged at his left side. "Why'd you do that?"

"Ow," said Humphrey, reacting to the push. "Why'd I do *what*?"

"Ow," said Hershel. "You! Stop doing that!" he said to Ned.

"I didn't do anything," Ned said truthfully.

"Ow," said Hugo.

"Ow," said Humphrey.

"Ow," said Hershel. At the last ow, Ned heard a dull thud and saw that a rock had landed in the dirt next to him. He realized the Ogre was being pelted with rocks.

"Ow," said Humphrey, and slugged Hugo.

"Stop it, ow, stop it," said Hershel. "They want us to fight and I'm not falling for their tricks."

"Ow," said Hugo and slugged back even harder. It really didn't matter what Hershel said. The other two started fighting in earnest as Tom increased his rock throwing, because it was Tom, hidden by some trees, who was throwing rocks and anything else he could find at the Ogre.

"We're saved by a magical rock rain!" cried one of the soldiers.

"No – it's not a magical rock rain! It's just Tom! Grab something and help," cried Ned, bending down to pick up a pine cone to throw at the Ogre. The soldiers, emboldened by Tom's success, finally started hurling objects, too.

Soon the Ogre, still fighting himself and trying to get away from the rocks and debris, stumbled backwards over one of the children's knapsacks and landed heavily, knocking their heads on the ground.

And, then, believe it or not, Duke Harry, stepped over to the Ogre, reached down and banged Hugo and Hershel against Humphrey's head in the middle, effectively knocking all three unconscious.

"That hand-to-hand combat really works!" he said in amazement, as Tom emerged from his hiding place.

"Tom, I didn't know you were such a good shot," said Ned, playfully punching him.

"I practiced last year so I could get even with Alf, without him being able to pull his magic on me," said Tom. "No more dresses for me, after that," he added slyly, and Ned groaned.

"The least you could have done is tell me about it too," said Ned. "Now I'm the one stuck being his laughing stock."

"Well, now you know," Tom laughed.

"I think we should use some of the braid to tie him – them – *whatever* they are, up," said Nell.

"Good idea," said Tom. The girls removed the braid from one of the bags and measured out a few lengths. Some of the soldiers wound it around the Ogre while the rest of the group quickly packed up their camp to get on their way. Although Lizzie could barely contain her excitement at finally returning to Zephram, she stopped to place three apples by the Ogre's heads in case they got hungry. And then they set off, none the worse from their most recent adventure.

"Now that we've got the horses, at least we don't have to worry that they can catch up with us this time," said Tom. Which was a good thing, because they had a feeling they just might run out of luck with Hershel Hugo Humphrey if they saw them again!

Chapter Twenty-Two

They covered a lot of countryside throughout the day after their early morning wake-up by the Ogre.

"I think we should stop pretty soon," Tom said, "and then we can travel closer to Zephram once it's dark. That way, we won't take any chances of someone seeing us."

"I think we're too late for that," Duke Harry said urgently. "Isn't that someone over *there*?"

"Oh, my goodness, it's the History Writer!" exclaimed Nell. Sure enough, hurrying across the ground to meet them, was indeed the History Writer, resplendent in his very unforgettable bright blue cape and tall pointed hat.

"But we're nowhere near his tree," said Ned, confused.

"Hey, you," called the History Writer, waving frantically. "Children, Duke Harry, over here, over here! I'm coming! I couldn't wait to find you. I've been keeping up with your history pages. I can't believe you've made it. Although frankly, I'm surprised you made it anywhere with these soldiers. Useless! Useless! I still can't believe what you've been able to do with them. When I read you were heading this way, I had to come to meet you."

"But you said you were too busy writing History to leave," Lizzie said, confused.

"Oh, the pens write themselves," the History Writer confessed. "I just collect the pages."

"He only wants to join us now because it looks like we might win," muttered Ned.

"I thought I could tell you what's been going on in Zephram, too," the History Writer said, knowing that would get their attention.

"What's happening?" asked Lizzie. "How are our parents and Zephera?"

"Everyone is still alive –" he stuttered to a stop when he saw Lizzie's shocked face. "I meant to say that everyone is just fine. Just, uh, stuck in the dungeons, eating bread and water. Standard prison type stuff, or so I've read."

"Well, this looks as good a place as any to stop," decided Tom, since the History Writer had effectively halted them in their tracks.

"What's in your bag? History pages?" asked Ned of the large duffle bag the History Writer dragged along behind him.

"Oh, those, yes, but I brought you some food, too. I thought you might be tired of all the apples and vegetables."

'Some' food turned out to be loaves of bread, some cheese, hard boiled eggs, and Ned's favorite, flora-ora butter.

In an instant, the children and the soldiers dove into his fresh supply of food. For awhile, all that could be heard was contented chewing.

"We could light a fire and toast the bread and cheese," Lizzie suggested at one point.

"That would take too much effort," Tom said.

"It's fine just the way it is," said Nell.

"Mhsmyns," said Ned, his mouth full.

When they were finished eating, there wasn't much to clean up at all. Really, just some egg shells. And, by now it was close to dusk. If they kept to their plan to travel closer to Zephram under cover of night, they would have to leave soon.

"So, History Writer, what will we find when we reach Zephram?" Duke Harry asked.

"Tomorrow the Month of Zephram Mondays is up, I'm sure you are aware."

"It's the perfect time for us to get there," marveled Lizzie.

"Prince Persius has planned a huge ceremony for the ransom payment."

"What's the ransom up to now?" asked Tom.

"The last pages I read the ransom was up to three million billion florites."

Duke Harry whistled. "But they can never raise that," he said.

"Of course not," agreed the History Writer, "but they're not meant to. Persius will never give up the kingdom, the flora-ora, or Princess Zephera now that he's gotten them all."

Duke Harry shot to his feet, his hand grabbing the sword he could now sort of use.

"He will never marry Zephera," he declared.

"Yeah, yeah, we know, we know," said Ned.

"Duke Harry, have no worries. Zephera's taken pretty good care of herself up until now," the History Writer said, chuckling. "She caused a stampede of pigs to run through the castle when he wanted to have dinner with her. She put dye in his water so his lips were blue for days. She rubbed poison ivy all over his chair so he got poison ivy all over his bu —" the History Writer stopped.

"Butt," supplied Ned, snickering.

"Bottom," said the History Writer sternly. "The Princess is quite a resourceful woman," he said to Duke Harry. "You are a lucky man. *If* you can stop Persius's wedding tomorrow."

"So what are we going to do, oh Big Brother King-to-be?" Ned asked Tom.

"What time is the meeting? And where is it?" Tom asked, ignoring him.

"The meeting is at 12:00, noon, in the castle courtyard, so everyone can see that the Zephram citizens failed to raise the ransom, and so that they have to watch poor Zephera's wedding. And I mean *everyone*. All the kings and queens and counts and dukes and guests from all around the world have been arriving for the Birthday Party and the Wedding."

"Wow, I never thought of that," said Ned.

"Obviously they didn't know about the invasion, and so as soon as they enter Zephram's gates, they're pounced on and led away to the dungeons," explained the History Writer.

"It was a pretty big guest list," Nell remembered.

"But, Persius's forces aren't *that* big. How can they capture everyone?" asked Tom.

"By surprise, just the way he captured everyone at the dinner in Zephram that evening," explained the History Writer. "The guests would never suspect that anything like this would happen to them when they come for the celebrations. Remember, you're the only ones who escaped from Zephram. No one else has, so word never got out about Persius's invasion. It's been incredibly easy for him to capture them all.

"Wow," said Ned again.

"And that means, children, Duke Harry, men, that you are the only hope left – Persius hasn't just taken over Zephram, why, he could take over the world!"

"So no pressure there," said Tom. "Okay, well, here's my plan." They all drew close to listen carefully.

"That sounds pretty simple," Nell said.

"Yeah, maybe too simple," Ned said, "because, you know, if we fail, Persius will probably take over the world, remember?"

"Got any better ideas?" asked Tom.

"I think it could work," said Lizzie, ever loyal.

"Thank you, Lizzie," Tom said, smiling at her. Then he turned to glare at his brother and other sister. "Well?" he asked pointedly.

"We'd better get going if we're to be there in time," Ned said, getting to his feet.

"Yeah. What are you waiting for?" asked Nell, getting on her horse. "Coming? Hurry up then," she said, and trotted off.

Chapter Twenty-Three

They rode several hours into the night, until they were back where their adventure started, hiding in the Royal Woods outside of the Royal Stables. They could hear the horses softly neighing in their stalls. Ned carefully stole through the shadows to find the poop door in the stable wall, and found good news when he peeked inside. Their tunnel was still hidden from view.

Coming from inside Zephram's walls they could hear raucous laughter and see light reflecting up into the night sky.

"Looks like they still don't know about the tunnel," Ned reported back.

"Great," Tom said. "Okay, the four of us are going back inside now. All we have to do is stay hidden and grab the Golden Ball in time for the ransom payment ceremony and Wedding at noon."

"That's all?" snorted Ned. "You really think it'll be that easy? Nothing's been that easy!"

"And, Duke Harry – right at noon you and the troops need to arrive," Tom continued, ignoring Ned. "Remember, you'll be pretending that you're all tired and dirty from your tournament."

"I'm certainly not pretending that we're dirty," said Duke Harry, and it said a lot about what they had learned, that he and his men were able to laugh over the destruction of their handsome uniforms!

"And remember, you're worried that your magic is gone," Nell pointed out helpfully.

"You can count on us to be there at noon. I just I hope my men and I aren't completely overwhelmed by Persius's men." Duke Harry admitted. "What good are we to you and the King then? You'll be right back where you started when Persius invaded."

"You have surprise completely on your side because you know what's really going on. They won't think you do," the History Writer pointed out. "And, remember, Duke Harry, that Persius won't expect you to be able to fight."

"Once we show we have the Golden Ball, I think the rest of the citizens will rise up." Tom said. "And that should be it. I mean, there might be a surprise or two –"

"Like the river," interrupted Ned.

"Like the Borneo Boar," added Lizzie.

"And Hugo Humphrey Hershel," said Nell.

"And the dragon … "

"And the ice field … "

"And –"

"Okay, I get it," Tom said. "Look, I'm doing the best I can. I don't see anyone else taking charge."

"You're doing great," Lizzie changed her tune.

"Enough talk, let's get going," said Ned. "Duke Harry, we'll see you at noon."

"Good luck to you all," said the History Writer. "I hope to see you and give you *these*," he pointed at the latest pages, "tomorrow!"

Chapter Twenty-Four

It was weird for the Royal Quadruplets to be back in their castle, because it felt the same and yet felt *very* different. So much had happened to them and to Zephram, but the physical surroundings hadn't changed except that Prince Persius's maroon flags (with the green serpents) were now everywhere.

Just as carefully as they had snuck *out* a month before, this time they snuck back *in*, darting from shadow to shadow, drape to drape, passageway to passageway. Ned led them again, just as he had when they escaped. There was only one really close call when they had to hide from a guard who was slowly pacing back and forth outside of their parents' Royal Bedroom. They sadly assumed that Prince Persius was now holed up there instead.

Eventually they ended up in the room that was probably the safest place for them to be, their old sanctuary, the Royal Schoolroom. It was, after all, one of the first places that was searched after the castle takeover, but since it appeared the quadruplets had perished from the Wild Hydrox 'attack,' they were relieved to see that Persius hadn't bothered posting a guard anywhere near it.

The Royal Schoolroom was dusty, dark and quiet. But it was theirs. The quadruplets stood within the darkness, taking comfort in seeing all their familiar things: the papers, the books, the telescope, the cushions, the games.

"Here we are," Tom said with a sigh of relief, as the girls plopped down on their chairs and Ned worked on lighting a candle with his stash of flint he took from a box in the bookshelf. "Okay, let's get Plan C started and find the Golden Ball."

"Plan C? I think Plan C was the raft," said Nell.

"Then Plan D was the Ogre," said Lizzie.

"Then Plan E was the Borneo Boar," said Ned, blowing carefully at the small flame he managed to make.

"Plan F was teaching the soldiers horseback riding and Plan –"

"Then this will be Plan Y and tomorrow will be Plan Z," Tom cut in. "Lizzie, can you bring me the globe from over on the shelf?"

"Plan Z has a nice ring to it," Nell said. "You know, Z, Zephram."

"Yeah, we get it," said Ned.

"Here's the globe. What do you need it for?" Lizzie asked, bringing it over to Tom at the table."

Tom carefully removed it from its stand. "You'll see. Can you give me the gold braid?" he asked. Nell opened up her knapsack and pulled out more of the gold braid saved from the soldiers' uniforms.

"Here it is. Why do you need it?"

"For this. I think it'll work perfectly," Tom said, laying a strand of the braid across the surface of the globe where it caught the candle light and shimmered.

"I get it," Nell said and put her index finger on the strand to keep it from slipping as Tom wound the braid around. Carefully, they wrapped yards of the braid around the globe, securing it here and there with small tacks and tape, until it resembled a very shabby, distant cousin of their own Golden Ball.

"I don't think we'll get them confused," Ned said, laughing.

"As long as everyone else confuses them, that's all that matters," said Tom.

Now, after coming so far with their rescue mission, the only things standing in the way of the success of Plan Y were actually finding the real Golden Ball and replacing it with this fake one.

"Okay, Ned, let's go find the Golden Ball."

"Ned? Aren't we all going?" Nell whined.

"No, we can't all go. We don't all want to be captured," Tom reminded her. "If Ned and I get caught, you two might still be able to help Mom and Dad when Duke Harry gets here. Don't worry, there will be plenty for everyone to do."

"Okay," said Lizzie, still annoyed.

"While you're waiting, if you think you're going to fall asleep, maybe you should do it in the cupboard just in case a guard checks in here and sees you asleep on your chair."

"Fine," grumbled Nell as the boys left.

Just on the off chance the Golden Ball was in its regular home up in the tower, Tom and Ned sneaked over there first. All they saw was the fluffy blue satin pillow with a big round indentation where it had peacefully rested and glowed for over a thousand years.

"Okay, then let's try the Royal Throne Room," whispered Tom. It wasn't there, either. As a spy mission, it wasn't very successful. How could they do Plan Y – *and* Plan Z – if they couldn't find the ball?

"He must have it in Mom and Dad's bedroom," Ned said grumpily. "I suppose we should have known it wouldn't be that easy to find."

"We'll have to wait until he leaves the room," said Tom. They hid behind some drapes that framed a doorway just down the hall from the Royal Bedroom, and watched the same guard they had almost run into earlier pace back and forth. Unfortunately, with many hours until daylight, they could be waiting *forever* for Prince Persius to leave the room.

"This could take awhile," Tom finally admitted. "We need to make a diversion to get everyone out."

"I have an idea," said Ned. "I'll meet you at the bedroom in a moment." Because he knew the castle so well, it was no problem for Ned to work his way through a couple of rooms, out windows, onto ledges, across balconies, and then come back inside farther down the hallway. Once there, he carefully pulled a wide panel of drapery into the low flame of a torch bracketed outside the doorway. In just a moment it started a nice fire. Ned let it take for a couple of seconds before yelling 'fire' and hightailing it out of the way of the ensuing commotion.

Prince Persius and his guards were among the many who poured out of rooms and down the hallway, to check the fire and put it out. It only took a moment to douse the flames, but it also only took a moment for the boys to check the Royal Bedroom and see that the Golden Ball was <u>not</u> there.

"Now what?" asked Ned.

"We keep looking," replied Tom. So look they did, from top to bottom, back to front, side to side. And the Golden Ball wasn't anywhere to be found – not in the Royal Game Room, or the Royal In-Door Swimming Pool, or Royal Stables, or the Royal Flora-ora Room, or the Royal Milk Shed or the Royal Kitchen, or the Royal Hospital or even the Royal Bathrooms. It was now past dawn, and the castle was stirring to life. It wouldn't be safe for the boys to search for much longer.

"It's got to be here. I can't believe he would send it off somewhere outside the walls. He would want it here where it would be safe with him."

"There is one place I can think of where no one would ever go," remembered Ned. "The tower above the Royal Dining Hall. You know, where *we* hid before the invasion."

"It's worth a look," agreed Tom. Sure enough, perched high up in the tower, the Golden Ball glowed, tantalizingly out of reach, on a ledge even higher than the balcony opening where they had hidden on the night of the invasion.

"Okay. There it is," said Tom.

"But we can't reach it," Ned pointed out.

"We can't, but I bet Nell can," Tom said.

Nell and Lizzie were just stirring in the cupboard when the boys arrived.

"I can't believe you've been sleeping," Ned said. "We've been so busy. We must have walked about 100 miles looking for that stupid Golden Ball."

"It's not like we had anything to do here in the dark," Nell said, yawning. "Did you find it?"

"Yep. Persius has it hidden way out of reach, up in the same tower where *we* hid at dinner that night," said Tom.

"So did you get it switched?" asked Nell.

"No, we weren't able to. It's too high," admitted Tom. "It's a ledge or two past that opening where we were."

"That high? We'll never be able to get it!" Lizzie wailed.

"*We*'re hoping *you* can, Nell. Do you think you'd be able to pull yourself up there and carry the fake ball to swap with the real one?" Tom asked her.

"Let me look at it, and I'll see if I can," Nell said. The quadruplets made their way carefully and quickly through the castle, and soon came to the tower. Now the girls had a chance to see the ball glowing above them, as they leaned out from their old hiding space and looked way above their heads.

"Hum," Nell considered. "Well, I think I can make it. Let me try. Lizzie, hand me some of the gold braid, I bet I can use that." Tom handed her the bag holding the fake ball, and Lizzie handed her the length of gold braid they had left.

Nell nimbly climbed up the inside grating of the tower while the others held their breath and crossed their fingers. Finally, she reached it and pulled herself onto the narrow ledge on which the Golden Ball rested. She pulled their fake gold ball out of the bag, swapped balls and carefully bundled up the real Golden Ball in the sack. She tied it closed with the braid and then lowered it down to her brothers and sister.

"Got it," Tom whispered. Nell quickly and carefully joined them a few moments later.

"That was *too* easy," said Nell. "Why didn't anyone else go up there and get it?"

"Easy for you, maybe," said Tom, "but I guess everyone was too scared without their magic."

"Okay, we got it, *now* what do we do?" asked Ned.

"Now we have to wait until noon when Duke Harry gets here and the ransom ceremony starts."

"Plan Z, remember?" Lizzie pointed out helpfully.

"Can we get something to eat while we're waiting?" Ned asked.

"If you must," Nell said.

"I'll meet you back at the Royal Schoolroom." Really, it was just like old times, sneaking into the Royal Kitchen for a snack. No one saw Ned back then, and no one saw him today, either.

"It helps when everyone thinks you don't exist," he said gleefully. Ironically, all he'd been able to grab were apples. Unfortunately, no flora-orasicles were around.

"After today, I will never eat another apple," declared Nell, but she chomped enthusiastically on hers.

"I think we should do something now instead of waiting," said Ned as he gazed at the bundle resting innocently on the Royal Schoolroom table.

"We can't. Remember, all we've got is surprise as our advantage," Tom said, disagreeing.

"But we've got the Golden Ball," Ned said.

"But *we* can't activate the magic," Tom reminded him. "Dad has to do that."

"Maybe we should just try to sneak it in to Dad," said Nell.

"Oh, that's a great idea! Do you think we could?" Lizzie asked excitedly.

"I don't think the Golden Ball will fit between the bars of the cell," Ned said. "But maybe if we got close enough to the cell and Dad saw us, he could put his arm through the bars and touch it."

"We could go try right now! Oh, what are we waiting for?" Lizzie cried. "They'll be so glad to see us!"

"And the guards will be glad to see us too," Tom said, "and they'll tackle you to the ground and take the Golden Ball back before you get anywhere near Dad."

"Spoil sport," muttered Nell. "I think they were great ideas. Beats sitting here."

"We're sticking to our Plan," said Tom sternly. "Just one more hour to go, that's all."

Chapter Twenty-Five

"Please," whined Lizzie.

"Please," whined Nell.

"Please," whined Ned.

"Oh, all right already," Tom groaned. After his brother and sisters wore him down with a half an hour of whining, Tom finally gave in and they left the Royal Schoolroom to sneak up to the top of the wall that surrounded the inner castle courtyard. The courtyard was where the History Writer had told them Prince Persius was going to ask King Hiram to pay Zephram's flora-ora ransom at noon.

They squatted next to several old cannons that hadn't been used for hundreds of years during these peaceful times, but were perfect for keeping them hidden from casual view.

"Now, isn't this better," Nell whispered, glad that she (and Ned and Lizzie) had gotten their way to move to the final destination of Plan Z a little earlier than Tom had wanted them to go.

"Just stay behind the canons and be quiet," Tom hissed.

"Now, if only the canons worked," said Ned wistfully.

Within fifteen minutes after they had taken their places, the courtyard started filling up with tired, dirty, discouraged Zephram townspeople, all burdened with their Month of Zephram Mondays' labor.

Bakers had bread, cheese makers had cheese, sausage makers had sausages, dressmakers had dresses, carpenters had benches, and shepherds brought their wool. It could have been like a big bustling Farmer's Market except that no one was laughing, no one was talking, and no one was happy.

One by one, the townspeople lined up in front of Prince Persius's men, who calculated a flora-ora florite amount for each contribution.

Suddenly there was a bustle of activity and the crowd parted to allow Prince Persius through. The children gasped when they saw their parents and sister following behind him, wearing handcuffs. Then came the poor Birthday and Wedding guests, who had unwittingly stumbled into Persius's trap. Then came Nordon and Fruston, the two treasonous advisors. Last, big ugly guards brought up the rear of the procession with all of Zephram's children: Alf, Amaralyn, teenagers, toddlers, and babies – all held to guarantee their parents' good behavior.

"Ah, my ransom," cried Prince Persius greedily. He grabbed a pastry off of a pile of baked goods as he passed it, and took a big bite.

"Deeeeeeee-licious!" he declared. "I don't know about all of you people, but I think I'm going to love Ransom Day! And now that I've got my hands on all of you," he cackled evilly, looking at his new, captive, noble guests, "I guess I'll be collecting ransoms from *every* country in the world. My brilliance astounds me when I think about it. Who would have thought taking one magic ball would have opened up so many possibilities for riches and world dominance? Hurry up with your counting," he ordered, and the clerks scratched away harder at their calculations.

Finally, the sun beat down directly overhead, and the clock in the Royal Clock Tower began to ring its 12 notes. The children looked at each other excitedly and anxiously. Noon time – rescue time – fight time – hero time – had finally come after one long month.

Except that it didn't.

"Where's Duke Harry?" hissed Nell, as the chimes faded away.

"Oh, man, do you suppose he can't tell time either? asked Ned. "It's not like he could do anything else?!"

"We'll have to give him a couple of minutes," Tom said, concerned. "No one's going anywhere. If they don't show up, we'll just do it." Uh, oh. What if they had to handle the rescue all by themselves?

"What's my flora-ora ransom?" yelled Prince Persius.

"It's short, Sire," came the sad, but expected, answer from the clerks.

"Short?" repeated Prince Persius, pretending to be surprised. "How could it be *short*? Hiram, I thought you were a rich country. I guess you'll all," he gestured expansively at the crowd, "just have to keep working. And I guess I'll just have to marry Zephera now."

"Leave my daughter and my people out of this," demanded King Hiram.

"HA, HA, HA, HA, HA," laughed Prince Persius. "Oh, Hiram, or, should I call you 'Dad,' you make me laugh!"

Suddenly, the sound of horses approaching the large gates was heard in the courtyard. The children looked at each other in relief.

"Hello, hello?" called out a hearty male voice – Duke Harry's voice. "Sorry we're late – can someone open the gates? May we come in?"

"Who is *that*?" Prince Persius asked King Hiram angrily, although the glow on Zephera's face should have been answer enough.

"Why, it must be Duke Harry," said King Hiram. "He *was* due back for the wedding," he added.

"*Don't* anyone say a word," demanded Prince Persius, "or you will be dead." He glared at King Hiram, Queen Melora, Zephera, the 'guests' and the townspeople. "Open the gates," he ordered his guardsmen.

"Zephera, my love," Duke Harry cried joyfully, as he and his men cantered into the courtyard, filthy dirty but surprisingly comfortable (to the children's eyes) in their saddles, and filled with enthusiasm and energy. "Sorry we're late. It was the stupidest thing, I hope you believe me, but our magic completely disappeared! It must have been some kind of flu that attacked all of us. That's why it's taken us a little longer to get back from the tournament. I trust we're in time. You're not angry with me, are you?"

"No," said Zephera faintly. Duke Harry quickly got off his horse to rush over to her. He stopped short when he saw her wrists were handcuffed.

"Why, what's this?" asked Duke Harry.

"This? Well, Zephera's sort of my prisoner," said Prince Persius, relishing every moment.

"What?" thundered Duke Harry. "Prisoner? Whose prisoner?"

"Why, again, that would be me," said Prince Persius helpfully. "But rest assured it pains me as much as you to see her in handcuffs, so she won't be a prisoner for much longer. She'll be my wife in just a few more minutes."

"Why will she be *your* wife?" asked Duke Harry. "She's going to be *my* wife."

"Because Zephera and her parents – actually the whole country here, *and* anyone who is anyone in the rest of the world – are my prisoners," said Prince Persius with great glee. "And, now, I'm sorry to tell you, it looks like you and your men are my prisoners, too. Guards, get them."

"I don't think so," said Duke Harry. He pulled his sword from his scabbard, and it glinted in the sunlight. Prince Persius laughed evilly.

"Oh, *I* don't think so," Prince Persius said. "Go ahead and try, I'd love to see it. But your magic's all gone, my funny little Duke. You're no match for my guards."

"Really," said Duke Harry. "We'll see about that. Ready, men?"

"Oh, *puleeeeeze*," drawled Prince Persius, as Duke Harry's men started to pull out their swords. "You're wasting my time when I could be rolling around in my big, lovely piles of florites. *And* getting married to the Princess. Nordon! Fruston!"

"Yes, Sire," answered the evil advisors.

"Do something with these soldiers, will you? Thank *you*!"

"Guards, take them!" yelled Nordon, gesturing for them to rush Duke Harry.

"Get them now!" yelled Fruston.

"Oh, *I* don't think so!" cried Duke Harry, and he and his men surged forward with a loud battle cry of "*Zephram!*"

Oh, it was a beautiful sight to Tom, Lizzie, Ned and Nell, watching hidden from high above the fray. Seeing Duke Harry and his men bravely and quite competently launch into battle against Persius and his men was almost beyond their wildest dreams of how this moment could have gone! They used all their new skills the quadruplets taught them – their swords, their fists, their fancy footwork – as they jabbed and danced in and out of the way of the enemy.

"How can this be?" Prince Persius demanded. "Guards, put an end to this foolishness. Get them. They're no match for you. I have their magic!" he thundered.

"No, *we* have our magic!" rang out a young, clear voice from above. All heads turned up to the parapets where Tom and his brother and sisters rose from hiding into view. There was a moment of surprised silence. Then –

"What – who – get them!" yelled Persius. Tom calmly pulled the magic Golden Ball from the burlap sack and raised it high above his head where it glinted in the noon-time sunlight.

When the Zephramites saw their beloved Golden Ball safe in the hands of their Prince Thomasin, they cheered, rallied and burst into action along side Duke Harry and his men.

It took a couple of seconds for Prince Persius to realize that something had changed with his whole invasion-takeover-riches-world dominance plan.

It may have been when the baker boldly banged him on the head with a baguette.

Or it may have been when the seamstress jabbed him with a big needle.

But it was for sure when Duke Harry struck King Hiram's outstretched hands with his sword and shattered the handcuffs.

Within 10 short, world-changing minutes, the tide had turned. Evil Prince Persius and his men were vanquished, and Zephram was saved! Their weapons were taken away, they were handcuffed and tied up, and then escorted under heavy guard to the Zephram dungeons: the very same dungeons that up until half an hour ago had housed King Hiram, Queen Melora, Princess Zephera and their important noble guests!

Meanwhile, the quadruplets ran quickly and joyfully through the castle passages to reach the courtyard and their parents, delightedly whooping and screeching and laughing and yelling all the way.

Of course, the first thing Queen Melora said when she saw the four Royal Children was, "Where have you been? We've been worried sick!"

"We went to get help," said Lizzie, as they threw themselves at their parents. Tom was still carefully holding the Golden Ball.

"Yuck," said Ned, as Duke Harry and Zephera started hugging and kissing.

"We've had such an adventure," said Nell, "oomph!" King Hiram had stretched his arms wide and squeezed the breath out of the four as he grabbed them all in a tight embrace.

"Thomasin, Nedwyn, I should have believed you," was the first thing King Hiram said to his sons. Tom handed the Golden Ball back to his dad, and as soon as King Hiram touched the Golden Ball, the magic coursed like electricity through the air, shocking all of the Zephramites as their magic returned to them.

"My boy, I can't thank you enough for rescuing us," said King Hiram, turning to Duke Harry and reaching out to shake his hand. "Your swordplay, your maneuvers – I'm amazed what you and your men could do without your magic."

"You're very welcome, King Hiram," said Duke Harry. "Of course, I would have done anything to protect you and the Queen and Zephera. And the rest of the country, and the world, of course," he hastily added, "but you should really thank Tom, Ned, Lizzie and Nell. Without magic, we couldn't do anything. Their

Highnesses taught us everything you saw here today and Tom planned the whole rescue."

"Children? What's this?" asked King Hiram of the Royal Quadruplets.

"It all started at dinner that night after we came to tell you Ned's story and you didn't believe us. So we hid up in the tower of the Royal Dinning Room to watch. Just in case there was any trouble. We saw Prince Persius's takeover, so we escaped to go find Duke Harry," started Tom.

"And then we went through the secret tunnel and the poop hatch in the Royal Stables," said Ned.

"We've got a secret tunnel?" asked Zephera.

"Yes," said Nell. "Didn't you know?"

"And then we got to the Rock Field and made it look like the Wild Hydrox ate us," continued Ned, and then Lizzie continued, and then Nell, and then Tom again, and so on and so on and so on.

"What a tale!" Queen Melora cried with delight when they finished. "Aren't you the clever ones!"

"I've got it all written down here, your Majesties," said a voice behind them. Everyone turned to see that the History Writer had arrived, long after the action was over, of course. He was holding out the long-delayed *History of Ancient Zephram* pages to King Hiram.

"So the prophecy was correct, that four royal children of Zephram would save Zephram and the world from a great evil," said King Hiram, shaking his head in amazement.

"And without a smidge of magic!" Lizzie brightly declared.

A murmur of 'no magic' rippled through the crowd of nobles and commoners and schoolchildren and workmen and bakers and carpenters and musicians – basically all of the whole assembled kingdom and guests. *No magic!* It couldn't be possible! And yet it must be, because they were *free.*

King Hiram stared very long and very hard at his four very dirty, very un-magical and very heroic children who he had always been afraid could be hurt or hindered because they *weren't* magical.

"Lords and ladies, fine citizens of Zephram," he announced in his big kingly voice, "through the bravery of your Crown Prince Thomasin, Prince Nedwyn, Princess Lizeta, Princess Elenlyn, Duke Harry and his soldiers, our liberation from Prince Persius has been achieved without any of the magic we use here every day. Today I issue this royal decree: Henceforth every Friday will be free of magic, so that we never lose sight of what was accomplished by all of you this past month, and of how our kingdom was saved!"

The happy crowd of Zephramites cheered their princes and princesses. And then they went on the cheer Duke Harry and his men, too! And then King Hiram, Queen Melora and Zephera. And remember Alf, the Royal Tailor's son? Even Alf came up to Ned and Tom and shook their hands. He was *that* excited to be *free*! (And Ned and Tom were so glad to be home, they even shook hands back!)

So what happened next?

First, Queen Melora had everyone bathe and clean up. (Even she was still wearing her dress from dinner a month ago!) And then the Royal Family, Duke Harry and his soldiers, the party and wedding guests and the freed Zephram nobles all sat down for a nice lunch that wasn't bread, flora-ora butter, water, apples or vegetable soup!

Then, believe it or not, right on time, the very next day, King Hiram celebrated his 50th birthday and Duke Harry and Princess Zephera were married in a grand ceremony.

How did they pull that off so quickly? Magic? Nope, it was *not* magic! For during that month of Zephram Mondays, the bakers had been baking, the seamstresses had been sewing, the florists had been arranging, the musicians had been orchestrating. Magic had nothing to do with it.

It was the most beautiful and extravagant day of celebration the country had ever seen. And with the whole invasion, imprisonment, and rescue theme, it was an experience that the guests from all over the world talked about for years to come.

As for Tom, Lizzie, Ned and Nell, well, of course the four un-magical Royal Children's exploits became the stuff of legends. But soon, the Royal Quadruplets found themselves back in the Royal Schoolroom, working on their lessons. Yuck – but at least there were no more dreaded *magic* lessons to worry about!

(And the other children were a *little* more fun to play with, now that they were impressed with what Tom, Lizzie, Ned and Nell had done.)

Understandably, soon after their big adventure, things started to get boring. Really boring. Until one day, the Royal Quadruplets realized that the reason everything was so boring was because everyone else but them was *repeating the same day over and over again.*

But *The Tale of Time Warp Tuesday* – well, that's a Zephram Tale that will have to be told another time.

The End